Arise and Walk

Arise and Walk

YURI NAGIBIN

Translated by
Catherine Porter

ff
faber and faber
LONDON · BOSTON

First published in Russian in 1987
in *Yunost* magazine

First published in English in 1990
by Faber and Faber Ltd
3 Queen Square London WC1N 3AU

Phototypeset by Wilmaset Birkenhead Wirral
Printed in England by
Clays Ltd St Ives plc

A CIP record for this book
is available from the British Library

ISBN 0-571-15455-7

1

A Journey I Never Made

I don't know if I loved my father in those early years. Probably not. I loved Dashura, our maid and janitor. Father, though, aroused my curiosity and awoke my fantasies. He would go off every morning, reappearing in the evening when the setting sun poured through the single window in the long corridor of our flat, flooding it with orange and throwing shining stripes on to the floor beneath it. The place to which Father disappeared was generally described as 'work', and sometimes 'the Stock Exchange'. I had no idea what any of this meant, but there was something magical for me in those last words, and until I went to school at the age of eight, and learnt to dissemble, if grown-ups asked me what I wanted to be when I was older, I would proudly reply: 'A stockbroker.'

I knew that there was a connection too between this mysterious 'Stock Exchange'* and the lovely banknotes I was given to play with. Children love playing shops – trading and bartering must surely be one of the most ancient human instincts. Staying in our dacha during the summer, we children would play at 'greengrocers' whenever it was fine: plantain leaves became lettuces, their green, pimpled shoots were cucumbers, and other plants were carrots, cabbages, parsley, turnips and beetroot. If it rained we would play 'bakers', patting mud into rolls, moulding wet sand into specially shaped cakes and pies

*The Stock Exchange officially existed at this time.

and 'baking' them. And during the winter we would play at ironmongers and hardware shops.

We didn't use bits of paper or metal discs for our shop games, but real money – crisp, pungent, red, blue and green patterned notes from the four corners of the earth. These old denominations gave me a thrilling sense of the limitless vastness of the world, and I imagined the Stock Exchange as both a port and a ship – or rather as the entrance into the breathtaking wide-open spaces of life. Father was a traveller, the only traveller in our family. Dashura went out shopping before I was up. Mother made her evening visits when I was already asleep. Only Father, with inexhaustible courage, vanished daily before my eyes into the unknown. And I longed to follow him there, into the world where all those crackling red, blue and green bank notes passed from hand to hand.

In our corridor, diagonally opposite the window that faced the sunset, there was a box-room. Two of its walls were proper structural walls, and the other two were just wallpapered boards, considerably lower than the ceiling. Whenever I had the urge to travel, those two fine steep walls became the sides of my ship. The sky beyond the window was the sea. The absurd little spired cupola of the Armenian church, which stood opposite our building, was whatever I wanted it to be: a lighthouse, an island, a town or a pirate vessel. And I was the captain of the good ship *Bourse* sailing off into the mysterious land of stock-brokers in search of my father. I had everything – a ship, a route, the sea, determination and purpose. The only thing I didn't have was the habit of abstraction, the capacity to dream.

I read only *Robinson Crusoe*, that most unromantic of travel books, packed with humdrum worries about food, clothing and equipment. Others might love this book for its sense of space, of wind and flight. But I, with my wretchedly literal imagination and indoor temperament, loved it for its domestic details: its endless lists of every conceivable object and dish, some of which Crusoe made, but most of which he salvaged from the sea or from shipwrecks. To this day, that book for me is a hymn to triumphant domesticity.

I never wondered what it might be like out at sea, between the stars and the ominous night waves. What I did know, however, from hanging about our kitchen, was the priceless value of a primus stove. Since I couldn't go to sea without one, I spent half a day constructing one from an old tin can, some buttons and wires. I had to be able to pump it or it wouldn't light, and after tackling this problem, I made further preparations. With a thoroughness which Crusoe himself would have envied, I laid in supplies of drinking water, pemmican, salt fish, ship biscuits, butter, matches, gunpowder, candles, clothes, sleeping-bags, paper, pencils and stamps. I even remembered my German grammar – at that time a German woman used to come to the house to give me lessons. For Crusoe, of course, mealtimes were the sacred rituals of his island existence, and I interrupted my labours only to eat my imaginary lunch. The complexities of preparing and consuming this lunch – woodchip stew and salad made from scraps of mother's green silk skirt – far outweighed that of any real mealtime. By the time I had finished, the window facing the sunset would be flooded with pink, then yellow, and red fires would blaze in the windows of the Armenian church, making it look even more like a lighthouse. I would be just on the point of giving orders to set sail, when a bell would ring in the kitchen, a door would slam, and hurrying past the side of my ship, swinging his mysteriously bulging briefcase, would go my father, a quick, cheerful man, with a dark face weathered by the southern winds. Father was back: he had returned on his own, without waiting for me, from the distant land of the stockbrokers.

'Dinner time!' I would hear my mother call, and glancing sadly around my beautifully equipped ship, its furled sails and stuffed holds poised to conquer the distances, I would alight on to dry land.

That journey was never made, but I made plenty later to make up for it, and covered many miles in my father's footsteps: to distant Irkutsk, to stuffy, dusty Saratov, to the miracle of Leningrad and to god-forsaken Egorevsk; to Kandalaksha, standing among hills covered in dwarf pine trees and lakes like splintered mirrors, to terrible Rokhma, lined like a school exercise-book with rows of barbed wire . . .

And there came the day once again when Father could not wait for me. He needed me and called to me, calling me for the last time, but I didn't furl my drooping sails and, unable to wait for me any longer, he set off for that final frontier from which there is no return.

2

How It Happened the First Time

By the time I was seven or eight years old, I already knew my father and loved him, even though he was only my third love. More than anyone else I loved Dashura, and after her came Mother. But my love for them was instinctive, not something I was aware of. Father I loved for the things I saw in him, and for the image of himself he presented to me.

Father was the strongest. One Sunday, when we had a lot of guests at our dacha in Akulovka, the men had a bit to drink and organized some feats of strength. Father lay on the grass and told seventeen-year-old Kolka Shugaev to get on top of him and pin him down. Kolka did as he was told, whereupon Father threw himself over on to his chest, with Kolka beneath him.

Father was the fastest. That same afternoon there was a running race, at which he beat everyone except a long-legged maths student called Mikhail Alexandrovich.

Father was the cleverest. Once he bought a huge watermelon at Pushkino station, and rolled it the entire three miles back to our dacha. True, when we cut into the cracked, crunchy ball we found nothing inside but a pink liquid pulp – but that didn't matter.

I wasn't bothered by the somewhat contradictory nature of my perceptions of him. It didn't surprise me that my strongman was unable to carry the melon from the station, and had to roll it back instead, or that the price he paid for coming second in the race was a slight heart attack. It wasn't a matter of self-deception,

I simply didn't register his small height, his almost female weakness and his clumsy, awkward hands.

What I saw in Father was supported by all the legends about him. He was tremendously brave: during the First World War he had been awarded two St George Crosses; he had once gone into a rifle charge, replacing his dead commander in battle. He was tremendously witty: of a certain acquaintance of his, who married a woman who wasn't quite as rich as he had imagined, he said: 'He married her for her money, but it turned out it was for love after all!' He was a tremendous card: one of Mother's admirers would always sit at the very edge of his chair whenever he came to visit. Once this man arrived with a bottle of champagne and, screwing up all his courage, he planted his entire backside on the chair and made himself comfortable. Father at once rushed down to the shops and returned festooned with bottles – he was even carrying one in his teeth. Putting the bottles down on the table, he sat down on two chairs and put his feet up on a third.

In short he was quite irresistible. A certain well-known Moscow authoress wrote a whole book about how much she had loved him, and how jealous she was of his feelings for her sister, who was even more famous and beautiful.

That was my father, then – strongman, athlete, warrior, wit, mad duellist, conqueror, hero. In other words, a normal father, the sort of father every young boy has, whom it is impossible not to admire, impossible not to adore.

Yet I reacted quite calmly to his first arrest. It happened on 8 February 1928, two days after Mother's name-day party, when we invited a lot of people round and ate pancakes. We had never had so many guests before, and hot clouds of thick white pancake smoke filled our huge flat like a steam bath. Next morning draughts swept through the rooms, as Mother went into every corner with the vacuum cleaner. By the following day all trace of the festivities had vanished, and life had returned to normal.

I woke up that night, something I never did normally, and sensed an unfamiliar smell, quite unlike the sweet, fresh smell in our flat: it was the peculiar, heavy, musty smell of soldiers' boots. I opened my eyes, and through the grille-like bars of my child's bed, I glimpsed the grey, great-coated back of a soldier, moving towards the door.

'Who's that, Mama?' I murmured sleepily.

'Go back to sleep, dear, it's Lyolya's brother,' whispered Dashura in my ear.

Lyolya was an old friend of Mother's, whose brother was doing his national service – or 'military duty', as my family still called it. Reassured, I went straight back to sleep.

Next morning I discovered that my father had been arrested. The grey soldier had come in the night with some other men I didn't know, and had arrested my papa.

I didn't really know what 'arrested' meant. All I knew was that he would be away for a while, that he had been put in prison, and that it was something bad. But though I could grasp all this rationally, deep down I was proud of what had happened: it wasn't every boy whose father was arrested, and I swaggered around the courtyard that day, spitting at the grey wilting February snowdrifts, and announcing to everyone I met: 'My dad's been arrested!'

I was an outsider amongst the kids in the courtyard, and I was painfully aware of this. I was the only one there from the intelligentsia, and they despised me for it. In a vain attempt to win their friendship I gave them my toys, coloured pencils, paints and even some elegant silver fruit knives. They willingly accepted my gifts, but refused to repay them with friendship. In vain I sulked at them for slighting me. I would swipe bottles and boxes from the wine warehouse. I would aim my catapult at people's windows, and at the big-buttocked dray horses who pulled the great hollow barrels to the warehouse. I would curse and swear like a regular drayman, and taunt the wretched old Jewish man from the next doorway. But it was no use. My antics were regarded with patronizing irony, or more often with contemptuous derision. I had imagined that my misfortune would at last destroy the invisible barriers between us, and that they would finally treat me as an equal; but all I got out of it was a brief, superficial curiosity, still tinged with irony. My suffering meant nothing to them – none of their fathers had been arrested.

I very soon became aware of the consequences of Father's arrest. On my way to the bathroom I had to pass through my grandfather's room. Every morning I would go to his bed, wish him good morning, kiss his prickly grey-bristled cheek, and be given twenty copecks. On Sundays it was a crackling new orange rouble note. The coins I collected in my money-box, the notes I gave Mother to keep. On the first Sunday after Father's arrest, however, after pecking Grandfather's bristly cheek, I saw with a sinking heart not the usual rainbow-patterned rouble note lying on the marble-topped bedside table, but a dim, dull twenty-copeck coin.

'Things are going to be harder now Papa's gone,' said Grandfather quietly.

Then I understood: this was for ever. The first joy of Sunday was gone for good. It was no joke when your dad was arrested . . . Did I know then what he'd been arrested for? I did and I didn't. At least I knew no less than I know now, all these years later. 'They're arresting all the stockbrokers,' was a phrase I heard over and over again in those dreadful days. People now had to get rid of those nice, brightly coloured pieces of paper I had always played with. But why couldn't they simply have shut down that mysterious place called the Stock Exchange, and taken the notes away so they wouldn't be any more use to us? How were we to know that what was allowed today would be a crime tomorrow?

At any rate, if anyone had to be arrested, it should never have been my father. There were those who really did gain wealth – or a decent living, anyway – from those bits of paper. Father got nothing, or next to nothing, from them. He played with them as innocently as I did, although with a great deal less enjoyment. No one in the world has ever been so utterly uninterested in money as my father. He was much too happy-go-lucky, too trusting, too soft-hearted and vulnerable, and he enjoyed life too much. He just turned up for work carrying his heavy briefcase, stuffed full of God knows what, while we were actually supported by Grandfather, who was a well-known doctor. So going without my Sunday rouble after Father's arrest was not really a matter of necessity, more of a ritual gesture, like putting ashes on one's head at a funeral.

I didn't spend a long time agonizing over the reasons for my father's arrest. I didn't suffer much, either. And Grandfather, Dashura and Mother filled the emptiness that followed his departure by redoubling their attentions to me. I still had my room, with its trapeze, its toys and the thick volumes of *The Three Musketeers;* I still had the courtyard, whose disturbing existence remained largely inaccessible to me. Beyond that was our wonderful dacha at Akulovka, with the winding river Ucha, its dreaming pine forests, its impenetrable alder thickets, and lanky Kolka Shugaev, who initiated me into the facts of life.

Just when I had almost forgotten Father, we met: our last meeting before he was deported to Siberia. He was given three years' 'open' regime there, which in those idyllic days seemed a terribly stiff sentence. Our meeting took place in Butyrki gaol. Mother, Grandfather and I hung about for some time outside its high walls, and were eventually let into an inner courtyard packed with people, like us, saying goodbye.

At a given signal, the whole crowd surged forward into a narrow, dimly lit tunnel, which I now realize was underground. Pushed forward by the crowd, we hurried, almost at a run, along the tunnel's clammy walls until suddenly those at the front came to a sharp halt and reeled back. Someone uttered a high-pitched shriek, there were screams, and more – men's voices, hoarse and terrible. The crowd raced forward again, a woman began to sob, and we found ourselves outside a barred gate leading into an inner prison corridor. Then we saw them.

At that moment I had the clear image of something I'd seen just a few days before. A rat-catcher had come to our flat and had put down a large cage in the box-room – previously my ship. Next day everyone in the building came out to watch him take away the cage, crammed to overflowing with rats. It looked as though the many-headed king of the fairy tale had fallen in. It was hard to believe that one trap could hold so many rats – a dense, squirming, squealing, reddish-grey ball of them, a wild tangle of tails, paws and triangular noses . . . It was this terrible, stuffy confusion of swarming bodies, battling arms and butting heads which greeted us behind the thick bars of the prison gate. They screamed, fought and howled, calling out to their loved ones on the other side of the cage, fighting their way forward to exchange just one glance, one word. And, suddenly, amongst these dark possessed figures with their wild, pale, terrible faces, I saw the swarthy, almost Oriental face of my father, filled with joy and suffering, yet struggling to retain its composure. He was standing just behind the grille itself. It happened quite by chance, as so often in a seething crowd of people, when those not part of the general mêlée end up at the front.

'Seryozha!' he cried, his voice breaking.

A sentry's jabbing rifle-butt imposed order on the jumble of prisoners. Father's face again flashed before me, then vanished, and once again we tore on.

After that we had a meeting behind two grilles separated by a narrow corridor, patrolled by a sentry. Mother managed none the less to slip Father some money – which was the only thing I remember about that meeting, since it was continually discussed thereafter as an act of great heroism, and the rest faded from my consciousness.

I never forgot my father after that. I carried his memory in my heart, and let nothing dislodge it. He returned to me as I had remembered him: strongman, athlete, soldier, wit, mad duellist, conqueror, hero. But now there was something else, which made my feelings for him far richer than other little boys' feelings for their far less remarkable fathers: he was suffering. This realization coloured my attitude to him for ever after with a delicate, almost morbid tenderness.

3

Irkutsk

In the brief time we lived together my father gave me no presents. True, on my birthday or at Christmas it was assumed that some presents were from Mama, and some from him. But I realized that this was a mere convention: all my presents were in fact chosen and bought by Mama, and Papa himself never gave me anything. Mother, Grandfather and Dashura all gave me presents, but Father never bothered. He lived avidly; he was still young and absorbed in his own life and, like most young fathers, he gave little thought to whether something might be too old or too young for me.

Family legend has it that when I took my first steps – things were hard for us at the time – I was rewarded with an emerald-green brocade coatee. Seeing me in this new outfit, Father nearly burst into tears, said I looked like a poisonous pod and immediately gave me his only jacket to wear instead.

I remembered this long after I had outgrown my smart coatee, and that was the last present I ever had from him. Yet when he was in poverty and exile he presented me with an entire town. And what a town it was, the gateway to the whole of Russia! I have already forgotten much of what happened later, but Irkutsk shines especially brightly in my memory. Every day I recall the details of our life in Irkutsk: there was nothing second-rate there, for nothing can ever be second-rate, even for a child, at these great turning-points of life. Irkutsk didn't merely shatter my old housebound existence: the little domestic creature that I was saw at last what a vast, complex and varied place the world was, and made the transition from youthful omnivorousness to a more selective appetite – in other words, he grew up.

All of life's immovable certainties collapsed on the journey out. We travelled from the warmth of Moscow in June to the snow of the Urals. Speechless, I looked out of the darkened window of the carriage at the dense scudding snowflakes. Then came the glades of morning, evenly covered in gleaming snow. Then, without transition or spring, came trees covered in fresh young leaves, while far beneath us, in the huge valleys between the mountains, lay blue-green coppices rippling like a river. There were also the real, mighty Siberian rivers – the Ob, the Enisei and the Irtysh – awe-inspiringly wide and mysteriously calm. As we crossed them, the train quietened, the wheels beat slower and fainter, and the carriages fell silent . . .

Irkutsk was a miracle, or rather a whole host of miracles. There was the icy Angara, in whose vast depths one could see every stone, every water-plant releasing inexhaustible streams of pearl-like little bubbles. We hired a catamaran, and rowed out to the little islands on the left of the harbour. When we reached the gulley between the two nearest islands, space turned round on its axis, the islands leapfrogged over each other, and the oars slipped from my hands. This dizzy spell lasted only a moment, and when it passed we discovered that we had fallen back a good ten yards. Between the two islands was a whirlpool with a powerful thrust, which swung our little boat round by centrifugal force, before hurling it back towards the harbour. We struggled against the current again and again, and finally, stupefied with blissful fatigue, we watched as some fishermen, armed with barge-poles, calmly manoeuvred their long, flat-bottomed pirogues across it.

Then there was the river Ushakovka, which ran into the

Angara. Its waters fell from the mountains with such headlong force that fishes swimming against the current sagged motionless, and you could pick them out with your hands or spear them with a fork. Swimming in its fast, warm water was a wonderful experience, like dreams of flying. I would swing my arms, barely touching the rushing torrent, and it would bear me with breathtaking speed to a wide estuary, where the waters of the Ushakovka and the Angara joined to create a smooth braking mechanism.

There were flowers, too, wild flowers growing on the slopes of the low mountains on the southern outskirts of the town – flowers it was hard to believe were real, they were so infinitely more magnificent than the modest little wild flowers of Moscow. There were flowers like fleshy cocks' combs, resembling the common snapdragon, but instead of red-stained yellow, these were of all colours, with blood-crimson upper parts, a bluish base, purple jaws, pale yellow brows, an amber head and yellow jowls. There was a flower like the everlasting flower, only it wasn't dry but quiveringly soft, every petal's orange wreath and blue crown containing a whole life of tender innocence. There were flowers like garden lilies – meadows filled with flaming, waxy lilies on long, graceful stems, with leaves like sabres. There were flowers which were like carnations but far more splendid, of every shade from violet to bordeaux. Then there were flowers that couldn't be compared or described, fantastic hybrids of cornflower and dahlia, nasturtium and camomile – fantastic fairy-tale flowers, with elongated pistils poking like tentacles out of deep, layered calyxes.

Father didn't know one flower from another. 'Must be a daisy,' he would remark thoughtfully, whenever we picked one.

Sometimes on the exposed surfaces of the mountains one

could see a vein of gleaming silvery rock. We would prize away a little piece without too much difficulty, rubbing off a fine shining skin rather like fish scales. 'That's micre,' Father would say. 'These are micre mountains.' And I would shiver with alarm at this first encounter with the origins of life . . .

Before that, in Akulovka, Mama had managed to show me a tree. This was one of the most important events of my life, more important than the first time I slept with a woman or the first time I was shot at – and far more important than anything I ever discovered from books. The tree was a craggy old weeping willow, its splayed-out branches crowned with a tangled mat of crows' nests.

'Look, what a lovely tree!' said Mama.

I looked at the tree, which I didn't see immediately, and then my heart stopped and I stood rooted to the ground, suddenly knowing with my whole being what a lovely tree it was, more lovely than anything else on earth – a whole pure, bright, free, happy world, which would neither betray nor deceive, but would rescue, support and cherish. It's very important for a child to see a proper native Russian tree.

In Irkutsk, living for the first time in my life so close to the rivers, mountains, rocks, trees and flowers, I felt overwhelmed by the mighty pressure of these feelings for nature . . .

From the roof of the long, narrow barn adjoining the house in which we lived, one could see the inn. Outside were rows of carts with broken shafts, and tied to the back of these carts were ponies with scraggy necks, swollen stomachs and veins as thick as rope, incessantly munching hay and trailing spittle from the corner of their black lips. Between the carts huddled terrible people with squashed, swarthy faces, hard round cheek-bones like fists, swollen slit eyes, and broad flattened noses. Many of them had no nose at all; some had just a black, rotten, gaping hole where their nose should have been; some had a white strip of bandage there, knotted on top of their head; and the luckier ones, who had kept the nostrils, had two long vertical holes. These were the Buryats, and they came in large numbers to our town. Dressed in linen shirts and fur-edged hats, accompanied occasionally by their noseless ear-ringed wives and their unbelievably dirty children, they would carouse all day at the inn, then collapse in a heap on to their carts, drinking vodka and cursing. I looked at them with curiosity, but without hostility. There was a sort of weird and eerie kinship between us. Their ghastly faces bore some kind of ancestral resemblance to my father's, the delicate face of my mother and my own. We came from the same stock. And with my new feeling for nature's expanses, flowers, rivers and mountains, I embraced my noseless brothers.

Mingling with the crowds on the town's high street, which led off our own Malaya Blinovskaya Street, were tall, elegant fair-haired men and similarly tall, loose-limbed women, wearing light cream or flannel outfits and lovely soft shoes with thick rubber soles. There was no sign of these people during the day; they only appeared after four, when the blazing light of day softened and the thick line of trees along the pavement threw off a cool, clear shade. Their easy, restrained gestures, their discreetly loud, confident voices and their open laughter sharply distinguished them from the rest of the crowd. They seemed encased in an invisible, transparent shield, accessible only to each other. I would see them playing tennis at the stadium, too, in white outfits and white caps with green celluloid peaks, curtly shouting, 'My serve!' or, 'Out!' Here too an invisible glass dome separated them from the spectators and from everything else in the world outside. They lived in their own universe, pure, vibrant and free. These fair-haired, long-limbed gods were employees at the Danish telegraph office. I was deeply disturbed by them, their complete disinterest in my life, their narrow, harmonious bodies, and their clear, expressive, sculpted faces.

During the first part of the day, when these gods lived hidden away from the world, I simply forgot about them. Life was so full of other wonders, such as the Irkutsk market . . .

Milling about amongst the countless booths, trays and wooden stalls was a bright, noisy polyglot crowd of Russians, Tatars, Buryats, Yakuts and Chinese. Whole bulls' carcasses hung from hooks, beneath which lay the horned, hairy, wide-eyed heads; there were elegant sheep's and rams' carcasses hanging up, and zinc trays piled high with tattered purplish-brown shreds of liver, taut, muscular hearts, and rough greenish-purple entrails, reeking of saltpetre. Next to these were wooden trays bearing dusty halva made from cedar nuts, clots of yellow creamery butter, and buckets full of pungent Russian butter, gold and grainy like semi-crystallized honey. There were lumps of aromatic resin, which looked like pieces of mountain rock and were very good to chew; mounds of various home-made sweets and little round pats of goat cheese; great hunks of crimson bear's meat, without muscle or bone, bottles of dark-yellow cream and cans of thick, rich milk.

The covered stalls were the kingdom of vegetables. Beets, swedes and turnips, as big as baby's heads, trailed their tops over the edges of the stalls like a peacock's tail; watermelons, split open like cups, sprawled on the ground; strings of onions rubbed their dead, desiccated skins against the live flesh of carrots, parsley, cucumbers, tomatoes and radishes, like dried flowers mingling with fresh. Huge buckets, filled with a dark swill which seemed to be sprouting yellowed dill-weed, exuded the delicious spicy smell of innumerable pickles; bunches of dry mushrooms hung next to dried pears, plums and apples – how good it all smelled under the hot Irkutsk sun!

Further off were the fish stalls, which gave off such a strong smell that you didn't go near them unless you had to. There were fresh fish, gleaming like silver, and smoked fish, like tarnished gold; and in the place of honour was the slowly expiring rich amber flesh of the Siberian salmon, the pride of Irkutsk.

The smell of foodstuffs blended with that of horses' urine, rotten hay and axle-grease melting in the sun; a hot, dense, aromatic cloud wafting over the market and pleasantly tickling one's nostrils.

We would wander, as though enchanted, amidst this profusion of delicacies, so fabulously within our reach; our bags would be stuffed with all sorts of things we didn't need, yet we would wander on in a trance amongst the booths, stalls and trays, unable to tear ourselves away. The market lured us on like a whirlpool, exciting us and tensing our emotions.

'Look at that woman with golden eyes!' my mother once exclaimed in a trembling voice, and the three of us pushed through the crowd, bumping into the trays and nearly knocking them over, until we halted in amazement before a pair of huge, golden, fairy-tale eyes.

I also recall the fine necks of camels swinging their haughty, resigned, fabulous heads over the rush and bustle of our market. I know this wasn't really so, and that the camels really came later, in Saratov, but I want to give them to Irkutsk. For they belong to the story of its market, not to Saratov's dusty, desolate market square, stripped bare by the great upheavals of mass collectivization.

Wandering around Irkutsk market were blind beggars and gypsies, organ-grinders and dancing bears; they sang songs about the tramp and the salmon barrel, and the mother-in-law who burns her step-children in the oven. After all these years I still dream of the bustle, the colour, the foods, the rich smells of warm, sticky tar and cedar-nut halva, and a woman's golden eyes.

But my hymn to the market would not be complete if I did not mention the first torments of love which befell me there.

One side of the square was occupied by private stalls, selling fish, meat, vegetables and confectionery. Arriving once rather late and not finding the cuts we wanted eleswhere, we tried one of these stalls instead. Behind a zinc counter covered in congealed clots of blood stood a young man with a thinning forehead and fine hair swept back over his crown and temples. He slapped a piece of meat on to the counter before his customers, then hurled it on to a carved wooden meat block, like an executioner's block, chopped through the bone and gristle with his axe, carelessly threw the chopped pieces on to the scales, and before the brass cups had had time to settle, so sure was he of his judgement, he bundled it all up in newspaper. He greeted Father as an old friend, but I was already so used to the fact that everyone in this enchanted town seemed to know him that I no longer felt any pride from these signs of friendship.

'Let me introduce you,' said Father, nudging me forward. 'This is our famous bicycle champion, comrade Tannenbaum.'

Tannenbaum smiled, made some response to these flattering words, and for some reason stretched out his bloody palms, but I neither heard nor understood anything. I looked dumbstruck at this great man, and a terrible, solemn music sounded in my ears.

Even then I was afflicted with dreams of bicycles. At home there was an old, faded photograph of my fifteen-year-old father, in open shirt, trousers and bicycle-clips, standing by a tree and gripping the handlebars of a bicycle, with the tip of his left boot just resting against the pedal. It was as though the photographer had just said: 'Ready!' and that Father, leaping on to his thin, horned, metallic god, was about to spin off past the trees into distant places inaccessible to mere pedestrians. I could gaze at this photograph for hours. It conjured up all the reined-in tension of Father's body: the sweating palms itching on the hot rubber handle-bar grips, the weight of the pedal tickling the heel – in a moment the trees would obediently fly past, squeezing their shadows under the wheels, with the golden arrows of the spokes flashing in all directions. The name of this metal god in my father's power was short and resonant as a gun-shot: 'Dux'. I knew there were other gods, too: the 'Enfield Rich', the 'Enfield Royal', the 'Enfield Ural', the 'Latvella', the 'Opel' and the 'BSA' – which I called the 'Beeser'. I would run several blocks in pursuit of a cyclist, merely to stammer out: 'Scuse me, mister, what make is yours?' I regarded anyone sitting astride the taut, heart-like saddle of a bike as a higher order of being. Imagine my feelings, then, on setting eyes on the king of this select breed.

Tannenbaum was not just the cycle champion of Irkutsk, but title-holder for the whole of Siberia – in other words, a major star in our sporting firmament. And so it was this champion who first introduced into my life the aching theme of second-best. I must have foreseen since childhood the secondary role I was destined forever to play in life. But even before realizing that I would always play second fiddle, I could never love the best either, and my heart invariably went out to the second-best: not Pushkin but Lermontov, not Tolstoy but Dostoevsky, not Alekhin but Capablanca, not Kachalov but Leonidov.

But why did it all start with Tannenbaum, who twice won the

Irkutsk championship, thus demonstrating before my eyes his supremacy over all rivals? A genuine, powerful love turns everyone into a prophet, even someone as young as I was. Despite appearances, I could never believe deep down that Tannenbaum's triumphs would last. Peering Cassandra-like through the mist of his triumphs, I could see imminent defeat – a hopeless 'second', where he would remain for the rest of his life. And so it was. I watched Tannenbaum beat the handsome young dark-legged Bataen, whose star was then on the ascendant, yet before the year was up this same Bataen had thrown him back into second place.

The doomed future of my chosen one merely strengthened my love for him. Every evening, with a sweet, aching excitement, I would sit at the back of the stadium watching his thin, crooked legs, pedalling desperately, stubbornly away . . .

It was a hard love. But I had another, too, which was happy, carefree and tender. Every morning I would dash to the corner of Malaya Blinovskaya Street and the high street, where there was a private photographic studio. In the window of the little workshop was a stand displaying photographic samples, and I would gaze at the round, sweet face of a young woman with smoothly brushed hair divided by a white arrow-like parting. Her bluish half-open mouth made sweet dimples in her dear plump cheeks, and her large grey eyes seemed intent on something good and happy. The low collar of her dress revealed a long, soft, round neck, and on her bosom she wore a little jewelled brooch depicting the Virgin's Assumption. She radiated purity, candour, goodness and femininity. People passing would stop at the window, and I imagined that they were all looking at Anya. They were probably curious to know the identity of this pretty young woman so full of cheerful kindness. What a pity none of them thought to ask me . . .

I would have told them she was Papa's friend, and mine too; that she had a soft voice and a quiet, steady laugh; that she had long, warm fingers, and that when she cautiously ran them through a man's hair, it would make him feel like laughing and crying at once. I wouldn't have told them that, of course. I would have said she was quite tall, taller than my father, and that when they walked down the street you would know that they had to be together, such was the bond between this slim woman and the small, lithe, sturdy, broad-shouldered man. I would have said, too, that she had an old father who had once been a teacher but was now a fisherman, and a large number of brothers and sisters; that their flat was crammed with nets and fishing-lines, with aquariums filled with gold and green fish and exhibits of stuffed birds and animals; and that I would have gladly spent the rest of my life with her, even as her youngest brother, amidst the marvellous clutter of this flat. I would have said nothing about the times, especially at night, when I would hear some great secret going on between her and Father. Yet I did not envy Father her love, and was happy to play my ordained role of third place in their affair.

For I didn't love only Anya; I loved tall, red-haired, shrill Zinaida Lvovna, too, though in a different, rather careless, disdainful way. Then there was a girl who swam across the icy Angara while we were in Irkutsk, although all I saw of her were her sunburnt arms flapping like wings in the foamy ice-green waves. There was also that woman with the golden eyes, who flashed across the market. I showered Father with all these women's affections – for they weren't any use to me. Father was the master of Irkutsk's miracles, and in those far-off days he was a magical being for me. Only much later, as we sat recalling the past one sad evening in the god-forsaken little town of Rokhma, did it emerge that he had indeed been loved by these women:

Anya, and Zinaida Lvovna, and the brave swimmer – even the woman with the golden eyes, who for Mama and me was never more than a fleeting vision . . .

I could never describe all the wonders of Irkutsk, yet I must mention just one more, perhaps relatively minor, event – when I got my own back on our Moscow courtyard, which had so stubbornly refused to accept me. The youngsters in our yard were never so alien to me as on those mysterious occasions when they chased pigeons. I couldn't understand the point of this game. Why did they whistle with three fingers when a flock fluttered from one cornice to another? Why did they spend hours on the roof of the woodshed, staring with an almost malign concentration at God knows what in the sky, then suddenly shouting and waving their arms? What was this pigeon-chasing in aid of? Was there really nothing more to it than driving a flock of pigeons from place to place? I sensed that there must be some secret purpose behind all this pointless activity, but I couldn't for the life of me think what. They didn't like outsiders spying on these sacred moments, and I could never bring myself to ask them.

It was in Irkutsk that all was finally revealed to me, for there I was no longer a pariah. The Keshkas and Lenkas – every child in Irkutsk seemed to be called either Keshka or Lenka – not only accepted me, they initiated me into their holiest secret, the pigeon chase. Above was the vast blue sky filled with pigeons of all colours – white, dove-coloured, skewbald and variegated, cuckoo-like tumblers, pure crimson mantises, pigeons belonging to no one, and pigeons who belonged to us or to the kids from the other yards. A flock of them would wheel across the blue sky, searching in vain for a place to settle, and would be chased away by the piercing shrieks and whistles of our pigeon-fanciers. Taking no part in the chase, I would crouch behind a tree, my sweaty hands gripping the end of a rope, whose other end was attached to the pull-up door of a little cage. Near this cage a blue female pigeon with clipped wings would strut unsteadily up and down. Now and then she would manage to fly a little way up, dropping two or three elegantly curved feathers, before landing again by the open door. The male pigeons, soaring across the sky, would suddenly swoop down, flutter over her house, and alight with a tapping sound next to the female. They would primly make the lady's acquaintance with their beaks, then follow her into the house, as though inspecting a flat for rent. I would anticipate this movement with a nervous jerk of my hand, the door would snap shut, and the pigeon was ours!

All these countless marvels, this highly-strung existence filled daily with new experiences, inevitably produced a major transformation within me. It happened shortly before we left, on the river Ushakovka, where I used to be sent off on my own to swim . . .

It was happy, spacious and extraordinarily bright there. The Irkutsk sun, reflected in the mirrors of two rivers, flooded the open spaces with a blinding light. The peaks of the micre mountains melted in its brightness, and the gleaming-white town seemed bathed in milk. There was so much sparkling, gleaming, shining, reflecting material on the Ushakovka promontory, it was as though blinding cymbals of the sun were being forged for the new dawn.

Once I stayed longer than usual at the river. I forgot the time, and dusk seemed to fall suddenly, borne in by a huge cloud hanging over the Angara. The expanse darkened and contracted. To the east towered the mountains, dull-grey and cold; to the west loomed the town, and the black domes of the churches. The sullen cloud and the unfriendly darkness of the encroaching park completed the encirclement. The water glimmered like tin-plate, and this spread weakly along the shore, like the shadow of a light.

I felt as though I were pressed to the base of a giant cup. Somewhere beyond its brim were Father and Mother, and my happy summer days in Irkutsk. But the sides of the cup rose higher and higher, greedily swallowing up the expanse, and a nameless fear entered my heart. Like a prisoner trying to break loose from his dungeon, I started searching for the weakest link in the encirclement. I took no hope from the mountains, the clouds or the park. Then I glanced at the town, where the highest dome of the cathedral harboured a pale gold light. I pressed three fingers together, struck myself on my forehead, chest and shoulders, and started passionately to pray.

'Dear, dear God, I love you so much, see that nothing happens to me, dear God, please see that nothing happens to me, and make sure I get back to Mama and Papa. Please dear God, I beg you . . .'

Those rickety black crosses and shabby domes became a focus of mystery and salvation for me. Humbly, ardently and hysterically I endowed them with all my newly awakened fear of life. It wasn't just the genesis of fear, but of the soul. At nine years of age I had bowed under the weight of my soul . . .

After this profound experience of God's power, I was constantly amazed by people's weakness. I realized that my guardian angels – my parents – could protect me only from crude everyday hardships, but were powerless in this world of fear and mystery. I saw how weak and indecisive they were, and how much they themselves needed defending, and I decided to become their guardian angel. From then on I never passed one dome, one cross, one door laying open the interior of a church, smelling of honey and coffers, without praying for some big or little happiness: 'Please, dearest God . . .'

Irkutsk had burdened my tenth year with these new and painful anxieties . . .

But all things must come to an end – the long Irkutsk summer was finally over, Mama and I again stepped into our compartment and the third whistle sounded. Standing bravely on the platform amidst the falling yellow leaves, joking inaudibly behind the thick windows, stood my poor father, no longer a magical being now, but simple, familiar and lost-looking, with wet eyes and a sad, thin smile on his Mongol face. I prayed passionately for his happiness, for his speedy return, and for everything to be all right. Blinded with tears, and convinced that he couldn't see me, I prayed openly, desperately and shamelessly, and the train moved off . . .

4

Saratov

When we went to Irkutsk, Papa had already served two years of his exile; before that he was in a desolate little Siberian village on the river Lena, near Kirensk, whose remoteness prevented us from seeing him.

From Irkutsk he was transferred to Novosibirsk. This gradual progression from very remote places to less remote ones was the result of Mama's tireless efforts on his behalf. The success of her regular petitioning would be marked by the appearance in our flat of two cheerful young lads, smelling of new boots and belt leather. One of them was dark, with a short pointed beard, and the other had flaming red hair and crazy, tender, pale blue eyes. The flat filled with exploding corks, loud voices, shuffling feet, laughter and the sounds of the gramophone, one of the first in Moscow, with its non-stop crooning of *'Was machst du mit dem Fuss, lieber Hans?'*

When Papa's three-year term of exile had expired, he was granted what was called an 'exemption' from certain towns. I don't remember which these were, but he gained little from his so-called remission. True, he could now live a little nearer to Moscow, but any towns remotely worth visiting remained out of bounds, apart still from those of Siberia. Why a man who had served his term of exile could not return home, and had to spend a further three years in exile, was a mystery. We grieved, we fumed, we wept, but we never questioned it. We would have been far more shocked if he *had* returned home. Then Mother set to work. The cheerful red-haired lad and his bearded friend reappeared, filling our flat with cheerful laughter and the fragrance of boot leather; once again corks shot up to the ceiling and the hoarse, urgent voice asked Hans what he was doing with his foot – and Father got permission to settle in Saratov.

Other boys had their fortunate fathers living with them and educating them daily with words, or with deeds and 'by hand', in Dickens's phrase, or with both words and deeds. My father too brought me up in a fashion, not through petty surveillance, but with towns, roads and the most poignant and soul-rending experiences.

Whereas Irkurtsk was all contrasts and diversity, my entire experience of Saratov passed in a single key, in the grip of a single consuming passion, which dominated all else – the Volga, which I never really 'discovered' for myself on that occasion, the town itself, which survives in my memory as a mere cloud of dust, and its people, with whom I had no contact. This passion was for butterflies. It seized me on the very day of my arrival, when the son of Papa's landlord showed me his collection, stored in two large flat cardboard boxes beneath a table bearing a children's game with the mysterious name of 'Richi-Rachi'. Pinned with outspread wings on to cardboard, the butterflies resembled the petals of a flower, the finest silk or velvet, or bright, colourful cotton. They were extraordinarily beautiful. I had never known there were so many of them, or such a variety of different kinds. I looked at them and I knew that from now on life would not be worth living if I didn't have my own collection. What was it about them that so fascinated me? Was it their beauty, or a premonition of the thrill of catching them, or someone else's infectious enthusiasm? Probably all of these things – but above all, the striving for completion and perfection inherent in all of us, unable to recreate our innermost self and seeking its form in something external. This passion for collecting is the focus for the dispersed personality to reassemble itself.

The master of the butterflies, sensing that I had been 'bitten', began excitedly to tell me about his treasures. There was the Urals Swallowtail, whose bright yellow wings elongated downwards into a graceful point, edged with a dark ringlet-like border. There was the White Swallowtail, which was even larger than the Urals one, but less prized. There was the Camberwell Beauty, whose velvety dark-brown wings were edged with black and white. There were two brightly coloured sisters: the Avanesse and the Avanesse Talent. There was the Marmoreal, whose wings were marked with a marble pattern. There were butterflies covered in little spots, the large Anthroceridae and the small Anthroceridae, which also came in orange and violet. There was the Large White, of the palest yellow with black markings. There was the Large Black and the Small Black, which looked as though they'd been rubbed with soot . . . I listened to the names, each one of which imprinted itself on my consciousness.

Having gone through the butterflies, the landlord's son passed on to moths, which occupied the second box.

'See how only their lower wings are coloured, and their wingcases are grey, so when they land on a tree trunk they make an envelope which blends in with the bark. Now here's a Pink Sphingida, and that's a blue one, and there's a Milky White, a real beauty! And this is the best of all . . .' He brought out of the table a cigarette box, and slowly opened it. 'A Death Head,' he said in a solemn, mysterious voice. 'Can you see the skull and crossbones?'

I gazed at the huge night flyer, with its plump waxy body, the black span of its upper wings and the delicate yellow of the round lower ones, and I was prepared to see not just a skull and crossbones but an entire cemetery . . .

The following morning, Mama helped me to mend a net (a shop net, the landlord's son remarked contemptuously, good only for catching caterpillars), and that was the start of the feverish, exhausting life in which I burned up the Saratov summer, all but burning up myself too in the process. The butterflies far exceeded all my Irkutsk passions put together – the flowers, Tannenbaum, Anya, Zinaida Lvovna, the Danes, the church domes.

I can only vaguely remember the Volga, and the sandy islands where we used to swim. All I remember is the wild rose bushes quivering with the little yellow frocks of the Lemons and the brighter dresses of the Large and Small Oranges. I have almost forgotten the street where we lived; all it means to me now is the flashing net in which I tried to catch a Large White. But I can remember perfectly each of the nine tram stops, as Saratov's nine holiday villages were called, which were connected to the town and to each other by a single-track suburban tram: it was there that I acquired by best specimens of butterflies and moths. Only the most basic examples of this winged species were to be found in the town and on the river.

At first we ventured only to the fifth stop. The trams came rarely and irregularly, and the further the stop, the worse the service. Sometimes there would be a breakdown, and a tram would be stuck for hours at the side of the road. With each trip we faced the threat of not getting back the same day. Yet we kept travelling further and further out, for the first stops yielded such paltry rewards, and what lay beyond was so enticing.

Our courage was rewarded. At the eighth stop, near a tiny pure spring peeping out of the grass like a dark bird's eye, I caught a slow, low soaring White Swallowtail with my net, and shortly afterwards its faster Urals brother. I had to run quite a bit after this agile, headstrong flyer, so unafraid of heights. Three or four times I lost sight of it, and once I was about to abandon the chase in despair. But then it soared up again in a ray of sun, like a teasing gold leaf, and once again I hurled myself after it. Finally, gasping, sweaty, dishevelled and happy, I stood before my parents, resting in the shade of the ditch, with my prey in my hands.

'Is that an Avanesse Talent?' inquired Father with a smile. He was no better judge of butterflies than he was of flowers, but I should have listened to the odd emphasis he placed on the name.

Despite all my labours, my collection grew slowly. Many butterflies were destroyed through my own ineptness. To be part of my collection a butterfly had first to be stretched out on to a sheet of cardboard with pins and thin strips of paper. But I would pull out the wings too roughly and they would collapse, or the strips of paper would rub off their fine dust, leaving them half-naked in the frame, or I would remove the pins too soon, so that the wings would fold up and, when I attempted to unglue them, they would fall apart. My first Swallowtails were destroyed in this way, as well as a large number of tiny, exceptionally delicate butterflies and a magnificent Camberwell Beauty. I was in such despair over this that Mama resolved to take me to the last, ninth stop, from where, Father assured us, no tram ever returned. There I acquired a new Camberwell Beauty, some new Swallowtails and even a Milk Sphingida.

This last stop deserves a special mention.

Father had little tolerance for Saratov's heat, and indeed any contact with nature generally made him ill. In the city he would be full of life and energy, but in the countryside he would immediately age, put on weight and gasp for breath. During our expeditions he usually slept somewhere in the shade, wheezing heavily with his mouth lolling open. When the ninth stop finally excluded all others, he no longer had the strength to accompany us, and Mama and I would go off on our own, sometimes disappearing for the whole day. This was cruel to Father, but it couldn't be helped – it was only at the ninth stop that Sphingidae were to be found.

Once Mama and I strayed a long way from the stop. Wandering into a grove of nut trees, we emerged into a wide country track leading into a pine forest. Tall, perfect masts of trees loomed up row upon row, and straight, bluish sunbeams, swirling with specks of dust, pierced their dense ranks like searchlights. Perhaps because these were the first pine trees I'd seen in Saratov, I immediately sensed that I was going to be in luck.

I looked for a strong stick, and moved along the edge of the forest, banging the trunks of the trees. They responded with a short resonant echo. Then a sweet chill ran down my spine as something dropped quivering from the branches and fluttered from the trunk, as though a large chunk of the bark had come to life; then lifting itself off the tree, it hovered in the air, flitted to another tree trunk and merged itself with that. There was a momentary flash of blue spots against the grey fluttering bark, and I knew for certain that this was a Milk Sphingida. I lunged at the tree on which it sat, but it had disguised itself so well that it was impossible to find. I banged my stick on the tree. The butterfly sat tight without giving itself away. And then a swarm of wild wasps nesting in the tree suddenly came out at me. I felt as though I was being inoculated for everything from smallpox to tetanus all at once. With a wild shriek I let go of my stick and rushed back to Mother on the road, losing my shoe as I went.

But the huge wasps, like sway-backed mares, buzzed above me frantically, attacking my head, neck and shoulders.

A man who was passing was touched by our plight and offered to retrieve my shoe. After many attempts, stung from head to foot, he beat the maddened wasps from their trophy. Then Mama begged a cigarette from the man and he went on his way, rubbing his bitten cheek.

'You know,' said Mama, nervously dragging on her cigarette, 'your Sphingida's still sitting there on that pine tree.'

I gazed fondly at my mad mother, and made for the tree.

We returned late that night, on some lost, errant tram. Father was waiting for us on the street, with a gloomy face.

'Papa!' I cried excitedly. 'Look what I've got!' And I showed him my Sphingida.

'Well I never, it's an Avanesse Talent!' he joked, forcing himself to smile.

But I didn't take pity on him. All I could think of was that my collection still lacked its crowning glory – the queen of the night, the eery, mysterious Death Head moth. The landlord's son explained that it could only be caught in the dark, by the light of a lantern. So began my nocturnal vigils. The moment dusk fell, I would go out with a large tin lantern and sit for hours in our wretched little back garden, where all the gnats and moths from the town would cluster around me and the lantern. The shadow of a larger moth would occasionally flash across the illuminated ground, making me start, and I would hear my heart still thumping long after it had gone. Towards midnight I would be driven inside to bed, for even my mother, who understood my torment, was implacable about this.

This consuming frenzy was rewarded with attacks of virtual lunacy. I would get up in my sleep and wander around with closed eyes, like a somnambulist. Several times I awoke by the bed of the landlord's son. His room was evidently the goal of these nocturnal wanderings, for there in a drawer in the writing desk was the cigarette box containing the Death Head. Did I really want to steal it? Luckily my moral impulses were still active, as well as my motor ones, for they would lead me away from crime in the nick of time, and deposit me back in my bed, away from my intended victim.

I don't know how it would all have ended if I hadn't suddenly and finally cooled towards butterflies. One day I showed my collection to a friend and fellow-exile of Papa's, who had a biology degree. He carefully examined my butterflies, then perched his spectacles on his nose and started reading the names which, like a genuine collector, I had attached to each specimen. A look of astonishment flashed across his face, then he burst into loud laughter, and took off his misted-up spectacles.

'Where *did* you get all this from?' he said, dabbing his cheeks with his handkerchief. 'I may be hopelessly out of date in this field, but why on earth has a Cabbage White been called a Large-Veined White? And what's an Avanesse Talent?' He repeated the name with relish, reminding me of the way Father had pronounced it. 'Do tell me where you got this classification from.'

'It's just what I was told,' I mumbled.

'Well you were told wrong. There are no such butterflies. There is a Vanessa Atalanta. *Avanesse* is simply an Armenian name. And this one here is of the Geometridae species, not the "Gomertida" – look, I'll write it down for you . . .'

I mechanically handed him pencils. The familiar names which I had taken into my heart disappeared, names which had been my hunting cry and had stretched my muscles and tensed my nerves when I would push, tired and sweaty, through prickly burdocks and nettles which stung me till I bled, in pursuit of some swift and agile fugitive. I hadn't caught a Camberwell Beauty at all, it appeared, but a Nun's Wing – it might have been a better specimen, but the discovery filled me with a sense of irrecoverable loss, as did all the Cabbage Whites, the silk moths, the Euprochs and Pyralidae, which replaced all my hard-won Sphingidae, Marmoreals and Large and Small Oranges. I looked indifferently at my collection, feeling stupid, pathetic and gullible . . .

Deliverance had come too late. When people ask me why I look so prematurely old, why my hair is grey, I gasp for breath and my face is so lined and dilapidated, why both I and my writing give the impression of exhaustion and virtual prostration, I can only reply that it all started with the butterflies. It was then that I realized that I had to live life at the limits; this realization was at first perhaps unconscious, and only assumed rational form later, when I no longer resisted these destructive impulses. At various times in my life the butterflies were transmuted into stamps, or *The Three Musketeers* (for years I lived a double life as both Seryozha and d'Artagnan), or billiards, or literature, or a woman. But every fresh incarnation of that first fantastic passion took me to the very brink of destruction.

Father sensed this destructive trait in my character. My obsessiveness was radically alien to his harmonious, easy-going nature. At first he tried gently to tease me out of my passion for butterflies. He then made a shy attempt to direct me towards less dangerous pursuits, such as the sports stadium and the circus, but he failed and gave up. From then to the end of his life he always treated me with a certain very slight caution and compassion. His caution sprang from his sense of Mother's dark side in me, rather than his own sunny nature; the compassion because he loved me, and his discovery of my inconstant, destructive nature was a tormenting grief to him.

Long after I stood on my own feet and was his one sure support, when one would have expected him to be delighted with his son for making the most of his inauspicious life, I would sometimes notice the same expression of pity on his face which I remembered from my childhood.

He loved me and was proud of me, but he didn't quite trust me. He didn't trust me when he read my books of short stories, or even the few favourable reviews they received, and he didn't trust me when I drove him around Moscow, sitting in my smart suit at the wheel of my own 'Pobeda' motor car. His scepticism was compounded by the fact that those of my stories which were published he considered rather feeble, whereas those that were rejected seemed to him, who was raised on the classics, to be deeply alien and distressing, filled with a hostile, perverse spirit inimical to an ordered inner life.

Things in life always happen in a complicated, indirect fashion. Sometimes – when he listened to my radio broadcast on the lofty rights of the Soviet citizen enshrined in the Stalin constitution, for instance, or when he read my article in the trade union newspaper about the tasks of planning – he would feel slightly reassured, and would start to treat me with a little more trust. But then I would shove some of my clandestine stories under his nose, and it would undo everything. My divorce, and the fact that I had no children, also frightened and grieved him, and reinforced his mistrust of me; it was simply more evidence of the same destructive spirit.

What poor Father didn't understand was that this destructive spirit was bound to lead me not to catastrophe but to the most commonplace life, ending my days with a respectable heart attack or cancer.

And however much I put on airs for his benefit, however hard I tried to present myself as strong, trustworthy and a fighter, an accurate judge of goals, tactics and timing, he saw through all my brilliant disguises to that sad, sweaty, obsessed boy, tormented by his pursuit of the unattainable.

5

Together and Apart

Before the end of Father's exile in Saratov, our flat was filled for the last time with the hoarse strains of 'Dear Hans'. This meant that Mother had rescued him from the last circle of Dante's hell, known as 'Minus Three', which barred prisoners who had served the second term of their sentence from settling in Moscow, Leningrad or Kiev.

I clearly remember the great day when we welcomed Father home. I had prepared myself for it for so long. At that time, butterflies and the timeworn Musketeers had been superseded by geography. I spent all the money Mama gave me on geographical maps. On my birthday and other holidays the only presents I would get were maps, atlases and globes, and maps and atlases were the tax exacted by Mother's friend, who subsequently became my step-father. The whole of my large, high-ceilinged room was festooned with maps. There were enormous maps, measuring several square yards, of the world and the five continents; maps of every country in the world, including the pigmy state of Andorra; a beautiful, brightly coloured map of the earth's fauna and flora, with a tiger pushing through the lianas, monkeys jumping from branch to branch, hippopotamuses, lions, rhinos, elephants, a lyre-bird, a platypus and a kangaroo; palm trees and dry icelandic moss, tropical forests and our own birch and alder thickets. The globes, from the tiny table one, the size of an orange, to the pale blue giant standing on the floor on its long black leg, gleamed like mirrors with the curved, bulging reflections of the windows. I am sure

Father would have been happy for the rest of his life with this expanse of the universe, imprisoned within the box of my room. But it was not to be: before him lay yet more terrible Russian expanses, where I was to follow him.

My closest friend then was a boy called Vadik, a slightly strange, mad boy, who was utterly devoted to me, and I prepared him to meet my father, this extraordinary man of legendary physical strength and amazing wit, a hero of the last war, and so on.

At last the day arrived for Mama, Dashura and me to set off for the Paveletsky station. I was on tenterhooks. I had imagined my hero stepping from the carriage with a chest covered in medals – and I would certainly have been terribly disappointed to see the small squat figure of my father in the flesh. But what faced us there shook me to the core. Terribly wizened, with hollow, grey sucked-in cheeks and glassy staring eyes, listless, disorientated and dressed in rags like a beggar – this was how my father emerged from the carriage, wearily dragging a filthy sack. We had learnt nothing from his restrained letters of how hard the past two years had been for him. He had known for a long time that his exile wouldn't end in Saratov, and he never believed that Mama would be able to do any more for him. Separation without end or limit had broken him physically and spiritually; he had given up.

I knew nothing of this then, but my grief would have been no less if I had. They had exchanged my father for another; I had been terribly and cruelly deceived. I rushed away from the station, and bumped into Vadik at the barrier; my friend had joined us, but had had the delicacy to keep his distance.

'Let's go home,' was all I said, running towards the tram stop, and with his usual extraordinary sensitivity Vadik forbore to ask me any questions . . .

At home, after Father had shaved, bathed, changed his clothes and resumed something of his former appearance, I still could not bear to go near him. I wouldn't look at him, I answered his questions in monosyllables, and kept trying to slip out of the room.

'Look how shy Seryozha is of you,' said Mama casually.

No, I wasn't shy of him, I was ashamed of this usurper, who had claimed the name and rights of my extraordinary father.

But later that evening, when he came to say good-night to me and kissed my head, and I felt his familiar touch and saw his small swarthy hand, so like my own, there was something so familiar and dear to me about him that with a suppressed sob I accepted once and for all this new changed figure of my father.

He didn't stay with us for long. Immediately he got back he was sent to the grandly named 'Novices' sanatorium for nervous and psychiatric illnesses, where he stayed for two months. Mama and I then left to spend the summer in the country. And that autumn, the moment we were together again as a family, they introduced the system of internal passports, and Father, as a former exile, was refused one.

He chose to make his home in the village of Bashkeevo, the centre of the peat-workings which served the Shatura electro-station. At that time it was in the middle of nowhere. The passenger train went only as far as Shatura, where one had to transfer to the workers' narrow-gauge line, then to the trucks of the little peat engine. We thought that Father would have chosen Kaluga, Tambov or some other town with direct connections to Moscow. But he chose the peat-bogs of Bashkeevo precisely because it *wasn't* a town. Shatura wasn't a town either, nor were the nearby settlements of Roshal and Cherusti. Moscow was the nearest town, and the Shatura region lay in the province of Moscow, so anyone living there would be quite entitled to consider themselves a Muscovite. Father recognized no towns but Moscow. He had a Slavophile's passion for it. But whereas the virginal Konstantin Aksakov beheld Moscow rather as an eternal bride, my sinful father regarded it as a woman with many faces, and the capital was for ever associated in his mind with the most stormy, romantic, triumphant period of his life.

Many years later, when I was an adult, I discovered Father's own geography of Moscow, and through it found new beauty in its boulevards, parks and sidestreets. When Father said 'Sokolniki', he saw not a dingy park, filled with beer kiosks, shabby cyclists and louts, but something like the Bois de Boulogne, under the shade of whose trees he had loved Elsa K. Clear Ponds – the nightmare of my childhood, where I was constantly being beaten up by the local bullies – were adorned with memories of his first great love, Lily K., the sister of Elsa. There was virtually no corner of the town which did not evoke some similar poetic response in him, and it was so as not to lose Sokolniki, Clear Ponds, the K. sisters and his happy youth that he chose Bashkeevo.

In Bashkeevo he quickly rose to the top. When he arrived, he worked as an ordinary economist, yet within a year he was head of the peat-works' economic planning department. He possessed a huge, hitherto untapped capacity for work, a clear, quick mind and modest ambitions, and he found the work fascinating.

In Bashkeevo, Father went through yet another unexpected transformation: he became an 'enthusiast', in the exalted sense in which the word was used amidst the hopes and aspirations of the second Five-year Plan. He didn't come to this speculatively, like others; he simply threw himself into his work, and for the first time in his life he felt committed to some genuine burning cause. He was helped in this by his good nature, an intellectual's capacity for sacrifice and his contempt for capitalism – the result of his youthful passion for Marxist philosophy.

During Father's five years in Bashkeevo we met irregularly and infrequently. He would work around the clock, then take three or four days' leave at once in order to visit Moscow. His visits were red-letter days for me. My step-father's hated comings and goings dispelled all the everyday routine of our life, all attempts at comfort and peace of mind. I was a creature of habit, and it delighted me that Father's arrival brought to our daily lives some of that sense of occasion which graces the life of real families, who imprint their own taste on such everyday events as an afternoon rest, a walk, a visit to a café, or bed-time, and for whom breakfast, lunch and supper are established rituals.

Father would arrive in the morning and, as if by magic, a huge, fluffy omelette with specks of finely chopped ham would appear on the table, as well as coffee with cream and a large, hot, flat bread (for some reason this bread has since vanished from my life). Then we would all sit down to eat, and Mama would announce that I wouldn't be going to school that day.

This was the other great joy of Father's visits. About the strongest emotion I knew then was a gloomy, intense loathing of school. It was like a love affair in reverse. I would strain every nerve to miss lessons, and my eternal battle with school literally destroyed my health. Father's arrival would free me from the struggle for a while, and what usually cost me so many torments and sickening stratagems would be mine for nothing.

Instead of school, Father and I would set off to the Museum of Fine Arts. The first time we ended up there by chance, but from then on these visits became a necessity for me. The museum and its contents transported me to a world infinitely remote from the rough world of school. The Fornarina, with her wonderful sheep-like eyes, simply could not exist in the same dimension as

Kaleriya Viktorovna, my hated class teacher, or the landscapes of Corot and Van Ruisdael with the landscape of Clear Ponds, where my school was. The cathedral silence of the museum's galleries shut out all the ugly chaos of the school timetable, and sad Watteau banished for ever the wretched anxieties of school, with its endless anticipation of new griefs and humiliations. I did not understand then what I understand now. I thought then that I worshipped art; in fact I just hated school.

Father cannot have enjoyed these trips very much. Art left him pretty cold, and he also tired very quickly. Yet he always suggested that we walk both there and back, if not to the house itself, then at least as far as Theatre Square. As we strode through the streets of Moscow, Father's face beamed with happiness. Winter or summer, in autumn slush or spring puddles, he always rejoiced in Moscow, always found a tender word for it. People were forever greeting him, and he himself was continually saying hello to friends, from a woman who had 'once been a great beauty', to an old barber who used to keep a special razor aside for him . . .

But looming ahead was the unforgettable year of Nineteen Hundred and Thirty-seven . . .

There is a legend, common to many societies, about a small island inhabited by a small, peaceable population, over whom hangs a terrible curse: that every year they must deliver the most beautiful of their maidens to a hundred-headed monster. A similar curse hung over our little family. Each successive official 'campaign' demanded that one of us be sacrificed. 1937 had no sooner dawned than my step-father was imprisoned: he became something of a John the Baptist of the Ezhov era.

Words like 'Lubyanka', 'treachery' and 'meeting' – the last word invariably accompanied by the words 'not permitted' – once again filled our house, like the bywords of my distant childhood. Father redoubled his concern for us, sending us almost all his earnings, including bonuses and holiday pay, which cannot have left him anything to live on himself. He also started to visit us more often, although when they started doing the quarterly accounts that spring, he couldn't come even for my birthday, and just sent me a letter and some money. So we were especially impatient for the May Day holiday to arrive. April 30 was a Sunday, and Dashura was up at the crack of dawn baking Papa's soft bread and preparing the eggs for his omelette. But he didn't come.

The train from Shatura arrived at eight-thirty in the morning, and it took less than half an hour to get to our house from the Kazan Station. At nine o'clock on the morning of 1 May, Mama, Father's brother Boris and I went out on to the balcony to wait for Father to appear around the corner of Telegraph Street. But ten o'clock came, and there was still no sign of him. We began to be seriously worried. At last I saw a familiar brown leather coat and grey cap in the distance.

'There he is!' I shouted.

'Don't talk nonsense!' said Uncle Boris sharply.

My eyes were much sharper than his, so why did I let his angry shout immediately convince me that I was wrong? The leather coat and grey cap approached and turned into someone unfamiliar, yet bearing an astounding resemblance to my father. The same height, the same walk, the same broad shoulders and back, but different . . . And yet he was so nearly my father. After all these years I am still haunted by an apparently inextinguishable sense of guilt that this man proved not to be my father. Had I just had a little more faith in miracles, had I just made just a little more effort, it could have been him. But I let myself be distracted, I was weak and cowardly, I didn't hang on long enough, and I let that dear man's fate slip from my hands.

We stayed out on the balcony for a long time. We waited for him until late that evening, knowing full well that he wouldn't have missed his visit to Moscow for anything. Every ring of the door bell, every noise in the hall, made us jump. We waited until the next day, and the next, and then the holiday was over. We deceived ourselves into being annoyed with Father for not sending a telegram to say he wouldn't be coming. Or we asked ourselves with worried faces whether he might be ill. Or if he had been delayed by his cursed quarterly accounts . . .

We continued with this pathetic game, played by people who are at their wits' end. But we already knew the worst. The only thing we didn't know was why.

After Mama and Uncle Boris had visited Bashkeevo, the reason became clear. Father had been arrested on 7 April in a pre-holiday purge which was to be a tradition for many years to come.

6

Fear

Mama and I were now on our own. In the mornings she would take money and parcels to my step-father in the Lubyanka, and petition the authorities in vain for meetings with him; the rest of the time her thin fingers forced the decrepit 'Underwood' typewriter to eke out a living for our little family. Unused to coping on her own, it wasn't long before she took the only possible way out. The doctors said 'malaria', but only because they needed to find a name for this disease from which she was literally melting away, like sugar in tea.

The mercury in the thermometer never went below 40 degrees, and for the first time in my life it occurred to me that I might be left alone in the world. Along with an immense pity for Mother, I felt a strange new power in myself – the power to end my life if she died. It was such a clear, straightforward feeling that, knowing as I did all the weakness and indecision lurking within me, I was amazed by the complexity of this nature of mine, which was capable of taking such decisions.

That was the start of my desire to explore the unknown world of my personality. The title of my first literary effort was the single letter 'I'. I very much liked writing about all the bad aspects of my character, all my weaknesses, inadequacies and sins, for they were all justified and illuminated by my recent decision.

It was about one in the morning and a deathly silence filled our large restless communal flat, when there was a ring at the front-door bell. 'It's for us,' my brain noted mechanically. Then I put down my pencil and pushed away the sheets of paper, covered in writing. Who could be visiting us at this time of night? Why was no one opening the door? The bell chimed again, firmly, but without irritation. 'It's for us,' I thought, smiling at the strangeness of it all.

Mother was lying in bed dead to the world, her hand flung back to her forehead. Her crooked arm was a whitish yellow, like the wing of a roast chicken, with incredibly fine bones jutting under the slightly pimply skin. That hand was especially hard to reconcile with what happened next.

I went out into the corridor. Utter silence from behind the neighbours' doors – they must sleep without breathing, I thought. The kitchen, lit by a single flickering lamp, looked vast, its corners plunged into darkness and its smoke-blackened ceiling like a gaping hole opening into the night. But the squat range, with its glazed white tiles, was cosy and friendly, and in the cracks between the tiles the cockroaches snuggled up asleep together. For some reason the sight of this stove completely robbed me of my courage.

I crossed myself, and whispered, as I'd done as a child: 'Dearest God, please make it not happen. Dearest God, you know how Mama is, please, for Mama's sake, do anything you want but not that . . .'

I fixed my eyes on the bell, smudged with soot and hanging there peacefully, as though it had never rung.

'Dear God . . .' I stopped, fired by a sudden hope. Then I saw the clapper lift, freeze for a second, and fall back towards the wall, briefly jingling against the metal.

'Dearest God, dear sweet God . . .' I gabbled, yelling out the words, while with three fingers pinched together I pounded at my forehead, chest and shoulders. '. . . Dearest God, if it has to be, if it really can't be helped, just let it not be me, make it not me, let it be Mama, dear God, but let it not be me . . .'

As though in reply, the bell rang once more, and to bring it all to an end, I undid the hook and flung open the door.

The landing, in the pale light of the moon, was deserted but for a cat, its two emerald eyes staring fixedly at the stairwell. The wind was slowly and silently lifting the frame of a window whose glass had been knocked out, and the bell-rope had caught on the catch and was twitching the bell.

The black well of the courtyard was silent and abandoned; only the top of the well was touched by the waning moon, and at the bottom the silvery circle of the home-made skating rink shimmered like a huge gob of spit.

Everything slept behind the darkened windows, and the world was safe again – yet it was a different place to the one I'd known just a few minutes ago.

I saw my face reflected in the window, a pink heartbreakingly familiar face looming out of the darkness. Yet it was another person's face, and I smiled at it with a strange, crooked smile which wasn't my own.

I was overcome by an aching sense of loss, and a bewildering sensation of freedom. There was only one other occasion in my life when I experienced a similar feeling – although in a much weaker, fainter form – and that was when I first slept with a woman. But my first experience of love contained none of the power and poignancy of regeneration which I experienced in that first betrayal.

It was that first serious adult fear at the kitchen door which revealed to me the real complexity of my nature. And that first, albeit imaginary, betrayal is a very important step on the road to maturity.

7

Egorevsk

We learnt that Father was in Egorevsk prison and, in July 1937, after months spent fruitlessly pleading with the authorities, Mother finally received permission to take him a parcel.

Having bought everything we needed to take, we travelled out to Egorevsk on a small suburban train reeking of disinfectant. For about five hours we crawled through the desolate countryside, still sweet with the freshness of new growth and lit by the still sun. As we passed the muddy glades and cuttings, the thin birch thickets and tiny stations, our mood was both sombre and elated, and we felt all the poetry of our solitude, our grief and our loyalty to the prisoners. Mama's face was thin, transparent and fragile after her illness, and every so often we smiled at each other, as though testing the bonds between us.

Leading from the station to the town was a mile of rickety wooden foot-planks, sagging under a layer of bright green mud. We made straight for the prison, which was housed in an old monastery on a fresh grass-covered mound. Around the prison, tacitly acknowledging it as their centre, were scattered the squat barracks and dreary little wooden houses of the town.

The whole of the green slope from the base of the mound to the walls of the monastery was scattered with our comrades in misfortune. There were sad ladies wearing old-fashioned straw hats with faded flowers, old Moscow intellectuals in pin-striped trousers and short light overcoats, and collective farm workers in baste shoes, who looked like local pilgrims. The whole of this disparate crowd was united by a silent, submissive bewilderment. No one knew if they would be allowed to hand in their parcels or not, but a rumour was listlessly going around that the director would be making his wishes known at five o'clock.

We wandered off to explore the town. I have seen many depressing central Russian towns in my life, but none has ever made such a joyless impression on me as Egorevsk. It was an ancient town, yet it was neither restful nor welcoming, without dreams or soul. It just seemed utterly bare and inhospitable. The houses were bare, without even any back gardens. The dusty streets were bare and treeless. The square by the cinema was as bare as a bald spot, with just a patch of trampled grass and some withered bushes bare of leaves. We sauntered along the wide deserted streets for a long time until we suddenly found ourselves in a small green oasis, bubbling with life. We were outside a large two-storey building, standing in the shade of some sweet-smelling old lime trees. It was cheerful, noisy and friendly there. On the door of the building was a metal plate bearing the inscription 'People's Court'.

We went in. The large ceremonial hall with its gilded chandelier was filled with people, and a case about child-support was in progress.

The respondent was a young lad with a stupid, pock-marked horse face. He was wearing a new jacket, and a tie whose knot seemed to be propping up his chin, and he bore himself with a careless masculine grace.

'I don't know anything,' he kept repeating, staring at the walls and ceiling. 'She and me were just good friends.'

The plaintiff, a thin woman with a yellow, frightened little face, was shy and hesitant, as if unable to believe that this magnificent toad had ever graced her with his friendship. She didn't cry, but the tears were quietly streaming down her face. When the woman judge asked her in what circumstances the respondent had made her pregnant, she replied almost inaudibly: 'On the bridge, and everywhere else, too!' And raising her head, she smiled for the first time.

But the most interesting person at this trial wasn't the couple, but a small, ragged, black-eyed girl, possibly a contract labourer, who was taking an unusually lively interest in everything that was going on. She was continually answering back, prompting the plaintiff, interrupting the respondent and finally picking an argument with the judge. The argument ended with the girl being fined twenty-five rubles, but even this didn't deter her, and no sooner had the judge gone off to a meeting than she bawled out to the respondent's wife, a fat, large-boned girl as pockmarked as her husband: 'You won't need your Kolka now, Manya! That'll be a quarter of your salary gone – fun doesn't come cheap these days!' Then turning to the woman sitting next to me, she said: 'Oh, I do love these trials! You get a real good look at other people's lives – it's just like your own!'

We went out on to the street again. We had no desire to see any more of the town: the prison and the court were the focus of its life. We dragged ourselves back to the prison. The green perimeter of its high stone walls was still scattered with people, most of them sleeping, others sitting or lying down, but all of them, even those asleep, clutching their parcels in their hands.

I looked at them, and wondered by what strange circumstance all these dissimilar people had been driven from every corner of Moscow province to this place. For some unknown reason, someone had cut the body of our nation in two, declaring one part of it guilty before the other. But the people languishing behind the stone wall knew as well as those waiting outside it that no one was guilty. The people guarding the prisoners knew it too, and so did those who had arrested them, and those who had accused them of crimes they had never committed; the people who were about to judge and sentence them knew it, and those who drove them into exile, and those armed with rifles who patrolled the barbed-wire perimeter of the camps. Everyone knew it, be they old or young, big or small, yet they still conspired to play this sinister game.

At about six in the evening the prison gates opened a few inches and the superintendent's voice barked: 'Let's have you, then!'

We were pushed and shoved forward, and we pushed and shoved back, in a frenzied and almost total silence. Along with all the others, we handed in our parcel, then feeling devastated and somehow cheated, we trudged back to the station.

At a sharp bend in the planked road, the monastery-prison suddenly came into full view, bathed in a pink sunset. For some reason it was only then, after spending the whole day at the prison, that I suddenly realized that my own father was there behind its walls, so near and yet so inaccessible, with his dark Mongol face, his smile, his little jokes, his small clumsy hands – that dear, poor man for whom I could do nothing, nothing, nothing.

Mama must have been feeling something similar, for she turned her face firmly away, but I saw the furrows on her cheek. After that came the long wait for the train, and the three lights flying at us out of the gathering gloom, and the fight for seats, and the darkness, and the stuffiness of the compartment, and our desperate tiredness when we got out, not knowing if we'd have the strength to get home. And then joy, the most stunning, extraordinary, unheard-of joy. Dashura opened the door to us. Looking unusually clean in a new apron, with her hair brushed and the fuzz on her upper lip shaved off, she silently flung open the door into Mama's room and the dazzling sight of the table laid with a white, stiffly starched cloth, and covered in all kinds of luxuries, with bottles of expensive wine gleaming amongst the soft caviare and chocolates. Before we had time to take all this in, who should step out of a dark corner of the room into the light but my step-father, released from prison and back in our lives and hearts again. Believing for the first time in the One to whom I had so often prayed, I strode over to the corner of the room, partitioned off by a cupboard, where a porcelain sink was fixed to the wall, and smote my forehead with three fingers, saying: 'Dearest God . . .!' But the words wouldn't come out, and laying my forehead against the cool smooth surface of the sink, I sobbed.

Three months later Father was tried. Trials, even those held in camera, were a rarity in those days. Such cases were usually settled in the torture chamber of the Lubyanka. Father had earned the honour of a trial because the evidence of his guilt was considered overwhelming.

In the days before the May Day holiday, Father was working flat out to finish his quarterly accounts. His colleagues were doing the usual pre-holiday loafing around, hanging up garlands, lamps, portraits, and so on. When they carried the third portrait into Father's office, he finally exploded with impatience, saying that quarterly accounts didn't get finished with portraits. And that was that . . .

The investigation dragged on – Father was also accused of setting fire to the peat-works. Although he was in Moscow at the time of the fire, the investigator stubbornly refused to accept this as evidence of his innocence. Father then developed a serious mental condition and was moved to an institute of forensic psychiatry, where they subjected him to the most rigorous tests, and even stuck needles into the poor man's body to remove some spinal fluid, before pronouncing him mentally fit. Meanwhile the investigator had fortunately found another 'arsonist' who hadn't managed to be ill, and he lost interest in Father, whose case then came before the court.

Mama, my step-father and Uncle Boris, who had spent the whole day outside the court, saw Father being led out after his case had been heard.

'Seven and four!' he yelled to them excitedly.

That meant seven years in a camp and four years' loss of rights. Before the door of the police van slammed shut, Father waved his sheepskin cap at them with the same happy expression on his face. He had been sure that they would sentence him to be shot.

8

Leningrad

In the winter of 1938 I received permission to visit Father, who was then in a camp near Kandalaksha, in a little town named Pinozero. Carrying two large suitcases loaded with warm clothes and nice things to eat, I left for Leningrad, from where I was to catch the 'Polar Arrow'.

As I set out on this distant journey – it wasn't so much a matter of the miles to be covered as the strangeness of my final destination on the Polar Circle – I was also setting out for the first time in my life alone, and with no real notion of how this meeting with my father would turn out. Over the past three years I had lost the habit of being with him; in those years I had grown from a child into a man, from a schoolboy into a student, and from a shy, struggling scribbler into a professional writer. I assumed that I should also find things in him which were new and unfamiliar to me. The meeting ahead was an equation with an unknown quantity, and I simply couldn't solve it. Sometimes, as lying on the top berth in the train, as it rushed through the snowy winter night, I would suddenly imagine myself meeting my old Moscow, Irkutsk, Saratov Papa, and I would be filled with feelings of warmth and tenderness. But then my treacherous ego would make some correction to this imaginary scene, and his familiar image would disintegrate and disappear, leaving a cold emptiness behind. In the end I simply stopped thinking about the purpose of my journey. I was merely travelling, why or where to I didn't know. The train rocked from side to side, shook, clanged the buffers, speeded up, then slowed down; lights flashed past the windows – and the movement, the rocking, the approaching and disappearing lights became the sole purpose of my trip. I knew nothing else.

I dozed off towards morning, and had hardly managed to get stuck into sleep when the doors banged, a blast of cold air blew through the carriage and the freezing cold woke me. 'We've arrived in Leningrad,' I thought.

Leaving my cases in the left-luggage office, I went out on to the station square and was amazed to find that it was an exact replica of the one in Moscow. Towns reveal themselves to people in different ways, sometimes at first glance, sometimes in the course of a whole lifetime. I was expecting a lot from Leningrad, and since this feeling is only one step removed from its opposite, I was disposed to dislike the town, and I unconsciously resisted the new turmoil Leningrad might bring into my life.

The station was like a shock-absorber, which immediately set the town in a recognizable context for me, and it was in a 'nothing to be scared of here' mood that I ventured on to the Nevsky Prospekt. Oddly enough, I made instinctively for the Nevsky and didn't confuse it with either the equally broad Ligovka or all the other streets leading from the station square. I also instinctively guessed the right direction to the Admiralty.

It was a grey, overcast day, like our early evenings in Moscow. I walked along the Nevsky, happy to be alone and my own master in this strange town, happy that it had accepted me so willingly and that, at worst, the familar station would open up that straight line, as long as the night, which led to a similar building in the world I already knew.

The independent, well-adjusted traveller will go to a café, order hot chocolate with cream and a ham and sausage omelette, eat, pay and go on his way with renewed confidence, afraid of nothing.

He will quietly enjoy Koldt's horses, and patronizingly acknowledge the Kazan Cathedral, but the gleam of the Admiralty spire, as it catches fire in the January murk, pierces his heart too painfully. He doesn't notice how his step quickens, his breathing becomes laboured, that he almost runs, bumping into passers-by and forgetting to apologize, that he is already transported by this town, and will be under its spell to the end of his days.

When I went to Leningrad, I expected to see beautiful palaces, cathedrals, columns and victory monuments. But I discovered something immeasurably more sublime: the town as imaginatively organized space. I was enraptured by the Admiralty, the Winter Palace, the Stock Exchange building and the arch of the General Staff. But what thrilled me even more than these buildings was what I discovered between them, in the expanse of the arch, in those endless vistas with which – I don't know how else to say it – Leningrad blesses one's every step. It's Leningrad's perspectives which are the most magnificent thing about it, these are what makes it inexhaustible. It is built not of stone – or not only of stone – but of water, air and sky, and these resources are infinitely renewable.

9

The Road to the North

The following morning found me on the middle berth in a third-class carriage of the 'Polar Arrow', without upholstery or sleeping-compartments. I opened my eyes and shut them again, almost blinded by the unbearably bright light piercing the carriage from every window. All around us, blazing in the naked glare of the sun, was an infinity of snow, not white but fiery and shimmering, throwing up shafts of gold. Every so often, the dazzling silver mirrors of ice-bound lakes outshone even the cruel brilliance of the snow. I recalled the purpose of my journey, and it seemed completely preposterous that all this gleaming emptiness, snow and ice, would deliver my father to me. In vain I tried to think about Leningrad – the light-filled emptiness around me wouldn't yield a fraction of its power over me. It had undivided authority over its victim, eliminating even memory itself. So I lay back without thoughts or feelings, as empty as the landscape, and before I knew it I had dropped off to sleep.

I slept for no more than an hour, but when I opened my eyes again my surroundings had changed beyond recognition. Beyond the windows lay greyish, faded drifts of snow, over which, like a continuation of it, sagged a dull white sky, a thin dark line of stunted pine trees, and little round coins of lakes, shimmering like silver foil. It was growing dark in the compartment and on the bottom berth, diagonally opposite me, a pilot in fur flying-boots was pawing at a thin young woman wearing a short jacket, a silk skirt which revealed the outline of her sharp knees, and a woollen shawl which had slipped down over her shoulders. The day before, when we were looking for our seats, I had exchanged a few words with this woman. She was travelling up from Saratov to meet her husband, who had just served his sentence in the Soroka camp, and Leningrad was her fourth change. Since she had no money for a bed, she had spent the night curled up like a ball on a bench, with her wicker basket tucked under her head. She still clutched this basket, filled with presents for her husband, twisting her fragile wrists to keep a grip on it.

The drunk, handsome pilot, breathing heavily, methodically went into the attack. He evidently knew that she would be getting out at Soroka, and that he had no time to lose. At first I naïvely thought that this resolute little woman would successfully repel all his advances. She hit his hands, pushed him off, jerked away her shoulders, and jumped up every so often with an angry face to stand by the window in the corridor. But then I observed that after each of these skirmishes, in which she seemed to me to be the outright winner, the pilot would have imperceptibly gained a few more inches of vital territory. After she had won another three or four rounds, one of his hands was moving across her bosom and fondling her small breasts, while the other hand was groping up her skirt. I waited for her to shout or call for help, and I started to rehearse my own part in the fight that would follow. But she just sat there quietly, looking out of the window with an expression of complete detachment on her face. Then suddenly she jumped up and went along the corridor to the observation platform. The pilot sighed loudly and followed her out.

When they returned, it was clear that she had won the final, decisive battle with the pilot. His red face was pale, his eyes damp and dropping with drowsiness, he puffed and yawned.

There no longer seemed to be any contact between them. He stretched out and immediately fell asleep, emitting a rich and sated snore, while she sorted through her basket with a distracted air, breaking off from this activity only to straighten the pilot's coat, which was slipping off.

Soon afterwards came the big station of Soroka, and a great crowd of men, smelling of frost, frantically surged on to the train, and the little woman's piercing sobbing cry of love, compassion and joy: 'Vasya . . .!' And a long, long embrace. Slinging the wicker basket on to his shoulder, stocky freckled little Vasya proudly escorted his faithful friend to the exit.

Now hillocks topped with tiny pine trees were racing past the window, the Polar Circle station flashed by, and I would soon be getting out. Yet I still had no idea how this barren, snowy wasteland might turn into my father.

Feeling as though I were playing some weird game, I dragged my cases on to the observation platform, and when the train drew into the little snow-covered station I jumped down. I had hardly glanced around when I was assailed by ringing female laughter and pretty young women's faces, fur coats and hats, silk stockings and galoshes. It was like a fairy story. This alien, hostile world suddenly enveloped me in a sweet, delicious female presence. Who were they and where did they come from, so lightly and gaily dressed? And what were they doing in this wretched place?

'Stand back, there!' shouted a voice, and a rifle-butt flashed before my face.

I dodged back. There was a large area between me and the flock of women, and from where I stood I could see that this area served to isolate them from everything else on the platform. This was no mere fancy: the entire brightly dressed, laughing, chattering flock of women was encircled by military escorts with fixed bayonets . . .

'Sergei Dmitrievich, sir!' said an ingratiating voice in my ear. 'Your dad sent me to get you.'

Before me stood a little peasant in a short fur coat, brand new felt boots and a cap trimmed with fox fur. With his broad cheekbones, thin beard and sly expression, he reminded me of a field-vole. Surprised by neither his appearance nor the fact that he knew my name, I asked him who these women were.

'Ah, we call them the Ukaze girls,' said the field-vole. 'The ones who were late for work . . . Give us your bags.'

I handed my cases to him. They had recently published an Ukaze recommending that people who were more than twenty minutes late for work should be punished with a year in a corrective labour camp. I had never imagined that this decree would be put into practice. And now I saw it in practice. I don't suppose these women had taken it seriously either, or they wouldn't have left wearing their silk stockings, short fur coats, fashionable little hats and light gloves. Perhaps they had been picked up straight from work? Well, even that was possible.

'They're laughing,' said the field-vole, nodding towards the women with an unpleasant smile.

We set off along a broad sledge track towards some darkening nearby buildings. There was nothing but emptiness, a little sun, and a scattering of low buildings – nothing particularly menacing, sinister or even strange about it. Then I noticed a beam of light running along something like a thread. This thread stretched between us and the nearest buildings; looking closer, I saw another thread above it, then another, and another. And suddenly the whole landscape was flashing with slender thread sunbeams, dancing and playing in front of us, to right and left and on into the distance beyond the hillocks and the tiny thicket of lilliputian pine trees. As we approached, the threads darkened, and I could see that there were about a dozen of them, stretched tightly on top of one another. And now it became clear that they weren't threads at all, but barbed wire, and that this sharp fence encircled the buildings towards which we were travelling. At that point I finally understood that the whole area was divided up like a chess-board into barbed-wire squares, and that spreading in front of me as far as the eye could see was a gigantic cage.

10

The Meeting

Checking my documents and filling out my pass to the camp zone took a long time. It grows dark early at the North Pole; the lights on the posts surrounding the commandant's office were switched on, and the round fish-eyes of the searchlights on top of the watchtowers were spreading their long beams into the ghostly bluish dusk, when a man in a short sheepskin coat, with a revolver at his side, ordered the patiently waiting field-vole: 'Go and get his father.'

The field-vole scurried off down the stairs, and the man with the revolver said to me: 'You can wait in the street. They'll bring him in a minute.'

I went out into the 'street' – a narrow corridor between two rows of barbed wire – put down my bags, and resigned myself to another long wait. But at this point everything happened at astonishing speed. From the sentry-post opposite the commandant's office darted a small man wearing a coat with a lambskin collar and a lambskin hat pushed back on his head; the sentry with his rifle waddled out after him, and scuttling after them came my friend the field-vole.

'Seryozha!' cried the man in the lambskin hat, bounding up to me as lightly as a young man.

We kissed. I recognized my father at once, of course, for he had changed little, although he looked a little older and greyer. But I wasn't ready to meet him. I hadn't been able to picture on the journey what our meeting would be like, I still couldn't imagine it once I was there, during the long wait at the commandant's office, and I felt inhibited by the presence of the sentry and the flitting field-vole. I felt myself becoming as stiff as a block of wood. I smiled woodenly, I turned round woodenly – I was almost angry with Father for being so fit, so cheerful, so unselfconsciously happy.

'Let me introduce you,' he said. 'This is comrade Lazutkin.'

The field-vole stretched out a frozen red claw from the depths of his sleeve.

'What a fine son I have, eh?' said Father, beaming lovingly at me.

'Very fine, sir,' Lazutkin assured him, winking at me for some reason.

'My son has come!' Father shouted to a passing man, who nodded and smiled.

'Come on now,' said the sentry.

'We're just coming!' said Father sharply, brushing him away. 'Stop bothering me! Can't you leave us in peace!'

A slave instinct stirred within me.

'Come on,' I said sullenly. 'There's no need for us to stand here.'

Father wanted us to stay here at the crossroads of the camp, so that everyone could see his extraordinary son, but he couldn't contradict the one he loved.

We went in: Lazutkin walking in front, weighed down with the bags, Father and me following, and the sentry bringing up the rear.

'Who is this Lazutkin?' I asked quietly. 'Your orderly?'

'Sort of. I feed and water him, and he does various little jobs for me.'

'He's a loathsome creature!'

'Oh, he's a frightful scoundrel,' Father agreed. He spoke without a hint of malice. He had lost none of his perceptiveness or his understanding of people; he had merely grasped the depths to which his associates might sink, and he didn't want to follow them there. This was not a sign of weakness, but of a generous and chivalrous nature.

'You'll never guess why he's here,' Father said.

'Murder?'

'No. Non-payment of alimony. He's a double bigamist. Belongs to some religious sect, you know. A fascinating character.'

'Should I give him something?'

'Don't for heaven's sake do that. Only yesterday he stole next month's allowance in advance.'

We had arrived at a little plywood hut standing apart from the long low barracks of the camp. The sentry undid the padlock.

'This is where you stay,' he said, then left, shouldering the sharp narrow gleam of his rifle.

Lazutkin dragged in the bags, and I switched on the light. A weak bulb under the ceiling dully illuminated some wooden beds, a plywood table with one leg, an iron stove with a chimney like a samovar, a pile of birch logs, a window coated in ice and walls fringed with hoar-frost.

Lazutkin stamped in the hall, blowing his nose loudly.

'Maybe we should give him a glass of something?' I suggested.

'You didn't bring any alcohol, did you?' my father asked anxiously. 'That's *strictly* against the rules!'

'To hell with the rules! I'm not going to throw away choice cognac and vintage port!'

'It'd be a shame to chuck it, of course. We must hide it.'

We started to argue, and I unfairly accused Father of cowardice. In his direct day-to-day contact with people he betrayed nothing of himself or his inner freedom, and this is a form of courage, but he had been accustomed ever since he was a child to respect the law. That was how he was brought up. I had been brought up differently. It had cost him a lot to argue with the sentry, while I had responded to him with slavish obedience, but for an abstract form of violence – the law – I had not the slightest respect. We settled our argument by agreeing not to hide the wine, but to drink it with Father's friends the next day, and to bury the cognac and the large bottle of eau-de-Cologne in the snow.

Slipping the eau-de-Cologne into my pocket and the cognac down my jacket, I set off with Lazutkin to 'work'. We were heading towards the barracks when suddenly the lilac tongue of the searchlight licked the sparkling whiteness of the snow.

'They've got us! Lie down!' Lazutkin shouted desperately.

We hurled ourselves into the snow, then crawled to one side, plunged into a ditch, picked ourselves up, made a short dash forward, spreadeagled out in the snow again, crawled forward again, fell again, and ran again, until Lazutkin said: 'That'll do! We can start digging now. This is a handy spot.'

It was 'handy' only for Lazutkin. When I returned to the plywood house I was quite unable to explain to Father where we had buried the cognac and the eau-de-Cologne.

'Never mind, Lazutkin will remember,' I said naïvely. It later transpired that it had 'slipped his mind' where they were. He had concocted that whole dodging game in the snow with the sole purpose of confusing me. Father must have realized this at once, although he showed no sign of it.

'That'll be all right, then!' he said, making a special effort to sound pleased. 'So here you are again!' And he kissed me with his cold, hard mouth.

I don't know why, but I started bustling about frantically,

opening up both the suitcases, pulling out food, warm pullovers and pants, and piling them on to the table.

'You must eat . . .' I said feverishly. 'Here's some ham, and some cheese . . . Shall we open the caviare?'

Father refused gently, saying he had just had his supper. The meals here were nothing special, he said, but the head of the planning department brought him food from the civilians' canteen. Nothing like the wonderful food I'd brought, of course, but quite filling and good all the same . . .

'*You* must be hungry, though, after your journey,' he said.

'No, I don't want anything – please eat something,' I begged him. 'Look at this roast veal Dashura made . . . and these socks Lipochka knitted specially for you . . .'

I thrust the veal and socks at him, wanting him there and then to eat up all the food and put on all the clothes. I needed to see with my own eyes that my journey hadn't been for nothing. What I did not realize was that my presence meant far more to him than all the treats, socks and pullovers. Than I came across the *Youth Almanac*, containing my first stories, and I thrust it at him, demanding that he read one called 'The Whip'. This minute, immediately.

'I've read it. It's a lovely story. Your Uncle Boris sent me the *Almanac*. It's a good thing you brought a second copy with you, though,' he added hurriedly. 'Mine's in tatters. You're the most popular writer here in Pinozero . . . But let's light the stove,' he said suddenly. 'Then we can have our feast.'

When he said that, I suddenly felt with every nerve in my body how cold it was. My feverish condition was caused partly by a lurking, unacknowledged fear that we wouldn't last long in our freezing plywood grave.

So we set to work on the stove. If there is some unsleeping eye which keeps watch on all human doings from on high, it must have been wet with tears at the sight of our feeble labours. No two people on earth have ever been more ill favoured by the material world as my father and I. Our hands, which were so similar and had never produced anything remotely useful in life, ineptly seized first the frozen blocks of wood, then the matches, then the bits of paper strewn over the floor. At first we crammed the stove's narrow mouth with whole logs, and tried to light them. But the matches went out the moment they touched the ice-encrusted wood. Then we stuffed in paper and lit that. The paper blazed up and died with a hiss, leaving behind an acrid stream of smoke.

'I know what,' said Father, masking his anxiety with a businesslike earnestness, 'let's chop the logs up into little bits, then it'll take.'

Beside the stove hung a blunt, rusty chopper without a handle. Father took a log, clumsily stood it on end and jabbed at it with the chopper. The log fell, and the chopper slipped from his numbed fingers and crashed to the floor.

'Let me try,' I said.

I managed with a great effort to chop off a tiny chip.

'Splendid!' said Father, admiring the chip. 'A real expert!'

After a few more chops Father had three or four slivers of wood in his hands.

'You have a rest,' he said, 'while I see to the stove.'

Removing the logs from the stove, he laid the chips crosswise, poked a bit of paper in and struck a match. The paper caught fire and the chips hissed and crackled with a cheerful little flame.

'There now!' he said, rubbing his hands. 'Our bungalow will soon be nice and cosy, then we can sit down for supper.'

I chopped off two or three more slivers. Then, I don't know why, perhaps the chopper got stuck in the wood, but it refused to go on chopping. I threw it aside and took another, but by then our chips had gone out, without even having caught fire.

'We need more paper,' said Father. 'This wood's completely frozen.'

All the food I'd brought was wrapped in several layers of paper, so we were well supplied with it, and a mound of paper was soon piled up beside the stove.

'You know, I think we could make ourselves perfectly warm with paper alone,' said Father.

We quickly filled the stove with this light reliable fuel, and soon had a splendid fire. How happily we watched the tongues of crackling flame bursting out of the stove! But a minute later all the paper had burned up, without producing any heat at all. I glanced at Father, and at once turned away again, for he looked as though he were on the verge of tears.

And then deliverance came. The flimsy door creaked icily and opened a crack to reveal a scrap of dense, vaguely stirring darkness. Such was the cold in our plywood home, though, that we didn't feel the icy breath of the night. The crack in the door then filled with a tall figure, and into the room stepped a man dressed in a short fur coat, boots and a warm cap with the ear-flaps down.

'Hello there!' said the man. 'It's like an ice-box in here – colder than outside. Are you trying to freeze your son to death?'

'The stove won't light,' mumbled Father sheepishly. 'Are you on guard?'

'That's right . . . I just heard your son had come, so I came to find out how you were getting on . . . Now get your things, I'm taking you to the bath-house, it's just been heated up for the Ukaze girls.'

'Really?' asked Father incredulously.

'Dmitrii!' the man stopped him sternly. 'What I say goes, OK?'

The guard was clearly showing off, and it was all being put on for me, a free man. For all my inexperience, I realized this at once, but I was so grateful to him that I even forgave him the over-familiar way he had addressed my father. I hastily threw all the food and clothes into the cases, and we stepped out into the silvery crunching snow. Fitful gleaming shadows played over the dark, almost starless sky, and I asked what they were. 'The northern lights,' Father mumbled from behind me.

The cold stuck my lips together, cut off my breath, stretched my skin tight over my cheekbones, pressed against my temples and froze my fingers, so that when we got to the bath-house I could no longer feel my face, hands or legs.

Our guide flung open one door, then another, and our eyes were struck by dense, blinding steam from the bath.

'The bitches!' cursed our guide. 'Still hanging about. I'll throw 'em out!'

As the steam drifted away, I realized to whom this was addressed. We were standing in the dressing-room, which was filled with naked and half-naked women. Some were wringing out their wet hair, others were rubbing themselves with thin towels, squeezing their shoulder-blades together to do up their brassieres or slipping skirts over their heads and pulling on stockings and trousers, while those who were already dressed were bundling up their dirty underwear. But none of them, whether half-naked or completely naked, paid the slightest attention to the three men who had just arrived. Not one of them turned around, or changed position, or stopped what they were doing. And when our saviour went up to them and ordered them to hurry up, they remained blind, deaf and dumb, with a complete and almost malignant indifference to their surroundings.

'Unhappy women,' said Father in a low voice. 'These are the ones who were late for work - the Ukaze girls.'

'But we came on the same train!' I said.

I couldn't help looking at the women again, but these silent, shameless bathers, with their coarse, wind-blown, sun-burnt faces, seemed to bear no resemblance to the bright merry flock I'd seen earlier on. And the clothes on those already dressed were rough, ugly and torn: coarse cotton underwear, cotton stockings, padded coats and thick leather or felt boots.

'No,' said Father, 'today's group have only just passed their medical. These are the old lags.'

'What are "old lags"?'

'The ones who've been here a long time.'

'I can see they have . . . The ones who came this morning were quite different,' I said. 'Like a garden of flowers.'

'These women looked like that when they came,' Father said sadly. 'They're put in with the criminals, and after a month you can't tell them apart. No clothes, no boots, no hopes, no standards . . . The only ones who more or less survive it are the ones who sleep with the camp bosses.'

While we were talking, our deliverer dragged out a trestle bed, rather like a sun-bed, only twice as wide, a straw-filled pallet, a plywood table like the one in our first shelter, and two stools.

'Suspicious hospitality,' remarked Father.

'Who is he?'

'Another scoundrel,' said Father thoughtfully, 'but in another class from Lazutkin. This one's in for armed robbery. He's almost served his sentence, and he's been made a junior guard for good behaviour. They often do that, but only with the criminals.'

Our criminal guard brought over a large hurricane lamp, put it down on the table and affably invited us to sit down.

Meanwhile the last Ukaze girl left the bath-house with a towel wrapped around her head. I supposed that we would now be left alone, but this was not to be.

Our benefactor removed his hat from his dark curls, which tumbled over his swarthy, chiselled features, and unbuttoning his coat he sat down at the table.

'And how is our capital city?' he asked me in a worldly tone.

It still shames me to recall what followed. I was completely possessed by the slave instinct which had stirred in me when Father had stood up to the sentry. It wasn't simply a matter of gratitude. This man, who personified both the prestige of power and the charm of the bandit, conquered, chastened and crushed me. Father no longer existed. Unable to hold his own in the giddy heights of our worldly conversation, he seemed to shrink into some distant past in the back of beyond. This bandit-guard's affability was not prompted merely by crude self-interest. He knew that I was a writer, and considering me thus to be someone of his own circle, he wanted to relax by chatting about various cultural issues he had long been deprived of.

'So what's new with Lyona?' he asked. 'Made any killings in Odessa?'

I had never been to one of Leonid Utesov's concerts in my life, but I have a fly-paper memory.

'He now performs at the new Central House of Culture. It's a huge hall, and you know the old man's voice. Although he does use a microphone, of course,' I said in a knowledgeable tone. 'He's doing a new programme now, about people in Moscow.'

'Any good songs?' asked my companion, screwing up his eyes.

'There's a blues number, "Dear Muscovites", but it hasn't got anywhere, it's not that good.'

'I hear Moscow's mad about Rozner,' he said with a smile.

I'd never actually seen Rozner either, but once again the fly-paper helped out.

'Ah, Rozner! The European school! The third greatest crooner in the world!'

'In my day,' Father intervened shyly, 'there was a singer called Stepovaya who was immensely popular. Is she still around?'

'Never heard of her,' I brushed him aside. 'Rachevsky is all the rage now.'

'They say he lives off his wife, Kapa,' my companion grinned. 'And how's old Varlamov? "In war and sorrow I sing of tomorrow . . ." '

' "Never ever lose heart . . ." ' I continued, imitating his voice. 'The old man's still alive, but that's about it.'

'Forgive me,' Father interposed again, 'but I thought Varlamov had died ages ago.'

'That was a different Varlamov!' I snapped and, to disguise my embarassment at Father's tactlessness, I started rummaging in my suitcase.

'Be my guest! This is all from Moscow!' and I loaded the table with tangerines, oranges, cheese, ham, bread, butter and caviare. 'Papa, entertain your guest . . .!'

Father reacted to my invitation without enthusiasm, muttered something beneath his breath, and even attempted to put some of the food back into the suitcase. I blushed with shame. But our guest, without appearing to notice Father's coolness, took a tangerine, peeled it and popped it in his mouth.

'You can't imagine how isolated we are here from real

culture,' he said. 'The minute I get back to Moscow I'll be straight off to the Hermitage Park!' He took another tangerine with his large strong fingers, and slipped the tender fruit out of its golden cover.

Father watched him tensely. I didn't know what to do. Then as luck would have it, two women entered the changing-room, one old, the other young, and both of them dressed in dark nun-like garments and dark shawls. Without saying a word, they dropped on to a bench and started unwinding their shawls.

'Hey girls,' shouted our guest. 'What are you doing here?'

The women continued to undress without replying, and he moved his large body from the table and went up to them.

'Can you really grudge him a tangerine?' I asked Father reproachfully.

'Of course I can,' he replied simply. 'Mama didn't spend a lot of time and money to feed that sponger.'

Having chased the women off, the guard returned to the table.

'Nuns,' he said casually, 'after a nice steam . . . Well, you have a rest, and I'll be off on my rounds. I'll lock the door so you won't be disturbed. Good-night.' And casually pocketing another tangerine, he went off.

The hurricane lamp went out, leaving only the weak bulb on the ceiling glimmering behind the congealing steam. The bath-house smelt of wet wood and soapy slime, but it was a nice warm smell, and it was warm lying under my coat beside Father, modestly pressing his thin body against the very edge of the bed. Everything bad, stupid, crude and petty vanished, leaving me with an infinite, heart-breaking tenderness for this dear body which had taken refuge beside me. It was a pure, true, childlike feeling. And just as when Father used to take me into his bed as a child, I cautiously and lovingly squeezed his shoulder.

'My little son,' he said, with terrible tenderness, and we fell asleep, having met at last . . .

11

A Day We Spent Together

It was one of the happiest days I ever spent with my father. Things went well from the start, when I successfully smuggled a bottle of wine over the sentry-post. The large litre bottle bulged visibly out of my coat, and Father worried that I would be caught, but the sentry clipped my pass without even looking at me, waved his hand – and I was through!

This part of the camp housed various offices, including the planning department where Father worked as an economist. He had his own desk, and he locked the bottle up in one of its drawers.

Gradually the other workers started to arrive, and Father got his own back on the previous day as he solemnly and happily introduced me to all his colleagues. At first I was embarrassed by this ceremony, but my new friends greeted me with such genuine, unaffected kindness and interest that I soon felt completely at home with them. I brought them a taste of the outside world, and their friendliness was directed not so much at me personally as at everything that lay beyond the barbed wire.

They did not envy Father, they were merely grateful to him for his emissary from the 'outside'. One man did show a personal interest in me, however. This was a junior economist named Guriev, a short, thickset man with a fabulous black beard spreading over his chest like a fan. He beckoned me to his desk, looked around furtively, then took out of a drawer a thick oilskin-bound notebook, leafed through it and handed it to me.

'But I didn't take the whip,' I read the beautifully penned lines. 'I didn't want to wield power over that fragile, unstable world, so close to suffering and death, where no force could bring back the life which one crack of the whip had destroyed.'

It was the ending to my story 'The Whip', and it made me feel agitated.

'You wrote that for us,' whispered Guriev. 'Your father calls my notebook "the intellect of cold reason and the heart of sorrowful observations." Inscribed in here is everything that's important.'

I still held the book. On the next page, in the same small clear hand, was another 'inscription':

In the vineyards of the Pyrenees
Some pages entertained a marquise
First they read her book,
Then they gave her a . . .

As well as this bearded gnome, the other workers in Father's office were a planner named Kharitonov, a tall clumsy man in a short, belted peasant 'Tolstoy' shirt, which he kept straightening out at the back, and a secretary-cum-typist, with a silly face and a nose like a button, but the most extraordinarily beautiful figure – it outraged me that such an intoxicatingly lovely body should be attached to that ridiculous pumpkin. She was a civilian and lived in the village, and when we were introduced she held my hand in hers, saying: 'We're having a dance in the club this evening.'

'Why don't you go?' suggested Father nobly.

Trying not to let my eyes wander below her weak-willed double chin, I firmly refused.

I also met the director of the department, another civilian, an elderly, rather deaf and very kind man. Not knowing how to express his regard for me, he dragged me into the buffet, where I bought a pile of sticky jam tarts.

Yes, it was a happy day, and it still shines especially brightly in my memory. Yet it is hard for me to say what exactly was so special about it.

I sat quietly beside Father as he worked. His small dark hands turned the handle of his arithmometer, deftly adjusted his slide-rule, clicked the beads on his abacus, then entered his calculations on to a sheet of graph paper. It was probably just ordinary, everyday work for him, but it seemed to me terribly demanding and important, way beyond the ability of anyone else in Pinozero. I loved his quick, accurate, confident way of working. Every so often he would break off from his calculations to ask me something about Moscow or the family, and I would reply briefly. It may seem strange, but neither of us had any particular desire for long, serious discussions; a few words were enough to tell us all we needed to know. It was enough that we were together, and that no one could separate us. There was a feeling of tremendous warmth between us, and everything seemed happy and harmonious. The sun through the window shone happily in the clear, bright sky, the old 'Underwood' typewriter tapped happily, and Guriev and Kharitonov cheerfully swapped jokes. My arrival had completely disrupted their usual routine, and these two middle-aged men, so sure of their own importance, became as skittish as kittens, dashing out of the room, teasing each other and the secretary, and interrupting each other to tell hoary old stories which made them roar with laughter.

Only one cloud marred this bright, happy day. When the lunch break arrived, the others went off to the canteen while

Father and I tucked into our Moscow sandwiches and the jam tarts from the buffet.

'There's one thing I've been meaning to ask you,' Father said, carefully scooping up the crumbs with his fingers. 'Were you and Mama ever taken into the internal prison?'

'What d'you mean?' I asked.

'In the Lubyanka, I mean.'

'No! Where did you get that idea from? They never even asked us to go there!'

'They showed you both to me,' said Father quietly. 'From a distance. Mama was sitting on a stone pedestal, remember, like those stone Armenian ones in front of our house, and you were standing right behind her . . .'

I looked at Father, and his face was far away. A moment ago he'd been sitting there beside me, familiar and dear to me in his every expression, his every movement, his kindly blinking eyes – and now, with his strange, half-open, staring eyes and tight, dry mouth, he seemed infinitely far away, and I couldn't follow him there. I suddenly felt afraid, and trying not to betray my fear, I said as carelessly as I could:

'What a ridiculous idea! They never told us to go anywhere!'

'I saw you there,' Father repeated in a lost voice. 'I just don't know if they really showed you to me, or if they faked it . . .'

'It must have been a hallucination, you were ill!'

'No, I was ill later. It was during the investigation I saw you, when they were accusing me of arson. They were trying to frighten me by saying they'd shoot you too if I didn't confess.'

'They never told us to go anywhere,' I repeated sullenly.

'Well let's drop it,' said Father gently.

I felt he didn't believe me, yet I was relieved that the conversation was over. I was terrified of what it might have revealed, and unprepared to shoulder a burden that might be too heavy for me. And I don't know to this day whether my father's strange vision was inspired simply by illness.

The director had got Father permission to stay out of his barracks until midnight. And that evening, when everyone had finished their working hours and their overtime, we organized a little banquet. The guests, apart from Father and me, were Kharitonov, who was on duty that night, and the faithful Lazutkin. Lazutkin dashed into the barracks for sandwiches, then stoked up the stove and hung up his coat in the window.

We had left the bottle under the table in the director's office, and we kept the bread, ham and cheese in our pockets. Then we discovered that we hadn't any glasses. We discussed sending Lazutkin out again, but this seemed too risky, since people in the camp missed nothing. So we decided to drink straight out of the bottle. We argued for a long time as to who should go into the director's office first. We all wanted Father to go, but he flatly refused. Finally Kharitonov resolutely straightened out his shirt at the back, and strode to the door. He was gone for such a long time that Father even ventured to suggest that our banquet might be over. But at that point Kharitonov returned, looking refreshed and a little flustered. It turned out that in our haste we had forgotten a corkscrew, and he had had to gouge out the cork with some scissors.

'A lovely little wine!' he said with emotion. 'You go now, Mitya!'

Father slipped to the door, and returned after a few moments, wiping his lips with his handkerchief.

'An excellent wine!' he said with the air of a connoisseur. 'Reminiscent of "Lacrimae Christi".'

Then it was my turn. Feeling strangely agitated, as though I were performing an act of great courage, I went into the office, took the bottle out of the desk and put it to my lips, anxious not to drink either too much or too little. Just one more swig, and another . . . My heart was flooded with tenderness and warmth. 'Dearest God, please make Father happy, please do this for me, dear God . . .' I put my lips to the bottle again, wiped my eyes and replaced the bottle beneath the table.

The faithful Lazutkin took a lot of persuading before he would finally agree to follow our example.

'I'm not that accustomed to wine, sir,' he kept saying, modestly putting his hand over his mouth. Despite this precaution, he gave off a strong smell of brandy and eau-de-Cologne, although in my emotional state it never occurred to me that he might have ransacked our hiding-place. He finally allowed himself to be persuaded, and emerged from the office crimson-faced, covered in sweat and rather befuddled. Port obviously does not mix well with brandy and eau-de-Cologne.

Kharitonov went out again, followed by Father, and then the much depleted bottle was in my hands again. I drank in small gulps, and every gulp produced a surge of noble and heroic feelings. I imagined myself endowed with immense power – derived from I don't know what, partly from literature, partly from some other source. I am travelling to the camp to take my father home. All the camp authorities pour out to greet me, while the inmates look on with hope and wonder. I summon up all my new-found power to lavish rewards on those who have been kind to my father, and to punish those who have not. 'Your plane is here!' announces the director of the camp, and Father and I walk towards our silver bird. The propellers roar, the security police salute, and we fly off to freedom and happiness . . .

Tears filled my eyes, the bottle was empty.

When I returned to our room, Kharitonov was munching a sandwich and telling a risqué story.

'D'you get it?' he kept asking Father.

My good, sensitive father got everything, of course, and when the flushed Kharitonov had delivered his triumphant punch-line, he said: 'That reminds me of an encounter I had back in 1923 . . .'

I tensed. I realized that he was about to retell something quite different to Kharitonov's coarse tale, and that it would sound outdated and provincial, like his questions the previous evening about the singer Stepovaya. It wasn't embarassment I felt this time, though, but a fierce desire to rebuff anyone who dared to patronize him. I glanced challengingly from Kharitonov to Lazutkin. My father had the right to be himself, there was no reason why he should bend to the prevailing crudity. But neither Kharitonov nor Lazutkin gave me cause to spring to his defence, and he successfully finished his story. And I realized then for the first time that he was a very much stronger, less vulnerable man than I had taken him for. He had clung to his old-fashioned ways as a form of protest, he had refused to adjust to his surroundings and would always remain true to himself.

Towards midnight the door opened slightly, and the crack revealed a flash of grey greatcoat and the familiar thrust of the rifle.

'Time, gentlemen, please!' said Lazutkin discreetly.

'Let's go!' Father responded cheerfully, kissing me, and adding quietly, 'What a fine son I have.'

At the door he turned round and jauntily snapped his fingers. With this uncharacteristic gesture he was showing me that everything was fine, that he had had a great drink, he wasn't at all downhearted, and he was going to bed in the best of spirits. My heart ached. I knew how hard it was for him to leave me for the night – and tomorrow we would be parting for a long, long time.

Kharitonov had just moved together the tables on which he and I were to sleep, when in came the cleaner, a young, dark-haired woman who looked like a gypsy.

'Can't you let me clean first, gov?' she said.

She was rather bony, but had a very pretty face, with large, dark brown eyes under thick lashes, glossy, arched brows and ripe, red lips. On her head she was wearing a cheesecloth bandage, which covered her right ear.

'Did someone run you over?' Kharitonov asked, poking his finger at the bandage.

'I was rolling in the snow with a bloke and got frostbite,' she replied defiantly.

Splashing water on to the floor from her bucket, she bent down and started mopping it up with a cloth. Her cotton skirt was pulled as tight as a bow-string between her straddled legs and full calves, which were tightly encased in short boots. Kharitonov crept up to her and tweaked her skirt. Without turning round, she slapped him with her wet cloth. Then, straightening up, she pushed a lock of hair off her crimson face with her crooked elbow, and said lazily: 'Get lost! I'm not going with *you*!' She turned her dark eyes on me, and added: 'I wouldn't mind that young one, though.'

'He doesn't need you,' Kharitonov said without malice. 'He's from outside.'

'From outside!' the woman said slowly, and a look of childish curiosity spread over her lovely, insolently lazy face. 'What's it like, then, out there?'

'You can't have forgotten!' said Kharitonov. 'It's not so long since you came!'

'I don't remember how long it's been,' she grinned. 'Since you lot came and started shouting, I haven't been able to remember a thing. Can't remember all the blokes, or how many I've slept with!'

'Where are you from?' I asked.

'The Southern Ukraine,' Kharitonov answered for her.

'I thought you were a gypsy.'

'Everyone thinks that,' the woman shrugged. 'I'm thin as a rake, just like a gypsy.'

'You're still in fine shape,' Kharitonov assured her. 'Have some cheese.'

'Get lost!' the woman repeated contemptuously. 'Cheese won't buy me! Nothing'll buy *me*!'

Kharitonov produced an uneaten sandwich from his pocket, then turning his pocket inside out, he collected some crumbs of bread and cheese in his palm and scattered them over the sandwich like salt.

'Have it.'

The woman cautiously accepted the sandwich and sank her white, even teeth into it.

I stretched out on the table with my hat under my head and my coat on top of me. Everything receded, leaving only Father's final farewell gesture, which followed me like a thread of pain into sleep. The table was very hard, and as I tossed and turned on it I drifted briefly awake.

'How can I, stupid?' I heard the woman say matter-of-factly. 'I haven't even done the corridor.'

'Come after the corridor, then. Clean the corridor, and come straight back.' Kharitonov was still clutching at his chance of happiness.

'All right, then.'

12

Departure

Next morning at midday I was sitting on my empty suitcase by the road to the station, gnawing on a piece of stale cheese from my pocket. An hour before, the time allotted for us to meet had elapsed, and I had had to leave the camp zone. But that wasn't the end. We were allowed to say our last farewell in the guard-house at half-past twelve, at the start of the lunchbreak.

The hours we had spent together that morning had slipped past with phenomenal speed. At first we seemed to have a superabundance of time, and we had sat quietly discussing all sorts of unrelated subjects, such as my first German teacher, Anna Fyodorovna, and our neighbours in our old flat on Armenian Street, and Furmanov Street, where Mama and I moved after Father's departure, and Guriev and Kharitonov. In other words, we had conversed like people with infinite time on their hands. We may also have been simply trying to spare each other, for it would have been too terrible to touch on what lay ahead.

Suddenly Lazutkin had poked his head round the door.

'I've brought the case,' he said, staring into space. I had to take back with me one of the two suitcases I'd brought.

'What, already?' Father said, getting his watch out of his pocket and for some reason starting to wind it.

Here too solidarity had helped us out. The main thing was not to see each other. As we stood together talking, even arguing – Father insisted that I take some food with me, and I flatly refused – it hadn't been easy to look without seeing. Not seeing or responding to the grimace of helplessness and pain on this dear man's face so as not to add to his suffering. But we had withstood the ordeal honourably.

I said goodbye to Father's director, to the bearded Guriev, to Kharitonov, Lazutkin and the secretary, and I went through all the necessary formalities at the sentry-post. Then I trudged off with my hateful empty suitcase, until a wind from the fields hit me in the chest and face and stopped me in my tracks. I sat down on my case with my back to the wind, and started looking at the barbed wire and the watchtowers, dotted about like mushrooms.

I was suddenly overcome by hunger. I had been bluffing when I told Father that I'd had lunch in the buffet; the buffet was closed that day for some reason, but I didn't want him to squander his Moscow provisions on me. I now painfully regretted the tangerines I'd fed to the guard, and the sandwiches I'd so generously handed out to Kharitonov and Lazutkin. Then I remembered some of my own cheese which I had left over from the journey, and I got it out, brushed off the dust and started gnawing at it. It tasted delicious, but it was so hard that even my strong teeth could hardly get through it. I gnawed at it till the very hour of our final farewell, which was announced by a shrill hoot, like someone whistling with two fingers.

The final parting started, like meeting all over again. We both arrived at the sentry-post and kissed, and Father said, as though seeing me for the first time:

'You look like a real young man now. It's the best time of your life – far better than childhood or adolescence.'

He then asked me what I would be doing when I got back to Moscow. I painted him a glowing picture of how I would be celebrating my holiday. I was going to the 'Sateevka' holiday home, where my girlfriend Liza was waiting for me, and where, as an acknowledged writer, I would have my own room. My life at the 'Sateevka' would be filled with love, skiing, billiards and a little writing. Father had to know that I would be fine, just fine, for this was the only way to make our parting bearable for him. Not to be outdone, he was going to sort through the books I'd brought him and draw up a reading programme, as well as polishing up his English. What a pity I couldn't stay in the barracks with him, he said, for I would have discovered what a wonderful place it was to study. In short, we were almost tripping each other up in our eagerness to describe all the urgent and interesting business that awaited us.

'Have you finished saying goodbye yet?' asked the guard standing beside us, and dropped his gun.

As the butt hit the rickety wooden floor with a muffled thud, it struck at my heart and I broke down. The tears started pouring down my face. Crying is usually preceded by some inner struggle, for consciously or unconsciously we always resist tears. But now it was as though someone else were weeping inside me.

The tears were pouring down Father's cheeks and nose, too, to his tortured, twisted mouth. We embraced and kissed each other's wet faces, kissed again, then rushed to our separate exits from the hut. As I left it, I saw him on the other side of the barbed-wire fence, followed by the foolish, futile sentry, stupidly thrusting out his rifle and struggling to keep up.

'Goodbye!' Father cried, coming up to the wire.

'Goodbye!' I cried, also running to the wire.

Someone yelled something from the watchtower, either at Father, or me, or both of us. We moved along the fence, separated by its six-foot quilt of barbed wire.

Some snowdrifts made me step sideways, and some invisible obstacle forced Father to dodge back from the fence, but still we walked on, keeping step and waving at each other. The road led me still further from the wire, and now I had to crane my neck to see him. And so I walked on, turning back to watch him following me, standing on tiptoe, or running forward into a gap, while the sentry lumbered after him, with his rifle under his arm. We went on, as though bound by an invisible chain, torturing each other and ourselves, yet unable to end it, until Father reached the end of his cage. Rows of barbed wire soared up in front of him, and he threw himself towards it to snatch one last glance at me. I could still see his face, but only dimly; then just the general outline of his figure, as though hanging from the wire; then just a dark speck between glittering threads, and this speck lingered on. It was still there as I approached the station, then it turned into a barely perceptible dot, more sensed than seen, and suddenly this dot vanished into a light halo surrounding the icy spikes of the wire.

I turned my face to the road and the wind. The wind froze the tears on my cheeks, covering them with a fine film of ice. And when I went into the station building to buy my ticket, my face melted and was as wet as though I'd just had a bath.

I had one more reminder of Father before I left. I had just taken my seat in the train when the stocky, thickset figure of the bearded Guriev popped up before me, laughing and stroking his beard, like a figure from a fairy tale.

'What are you doing here?' I said.

'They're sending me to Kandalaksha,' said the gnome happily.

'How is Father? How is he feeling?'

'He doesn't let on . . .' Guriev replied mysteriously. 'He wanted me to take a packet of fruit drops for you, but I left them behind.' He laughed quietly again.

I imagined Father slipping the clumsily wrapped packet of

fruit drops into Guriev's pocket, and how much this last pathetic kindness to his son must have meant to him.

'Better if he eats them, eh?' said Guriev, evidently proud of what he had done.

I had no reason to contradict him, he had done it out of kindness to Father, but those fruit drops were the final blow. All the way to Moscow I lay on the upper berth with my wet face buried in the dusty cushion. I don't know what it was about that packet. If it hadn't been that, it would have been something else. Can there be any limit to human pain?

13

Years Later

When I left Father in December 1940, I had no doubt that I would see him again in a year at the latest. But on that unforgettable June morning in 1941 which proclaimed the dread word 'War', I mentally said goodbye to him for ever. Amongst all the losses of war – and at the very start I lost my two best, and perhaps only, friends – my first loss was my father. How could the political prisoners in the camps be expected to survive, when the capital itself was beset by food shortages from the very start? And the Soroka camps were near the border, in the immediate firing line.

'We won't see Mitya again,' said Mother, shaking her head with a strange half-smile on her face.

We said no more about it. The war was for real, it demanded blood and more blood, millions of gallons of blood – young or old, fresh or putrid, it wasn't choosy, it rushed on, allowing no time for grief or reflection. But for the blood of a political prisoner's son it had no use. When the Rostokin recruitment office announced that they were enrolling students for the lieutenants' school, I hurried straight over. But they had already discovered that my father was in a camp, and tactfully suggested that I study elsewhere. Poor idiot that I was, I had wanted to expiate with my blood a crime my father had never committed! I should have remembered that I was very nearly thrown out of the institute, after someone informed the authorities that my father was inside. For the purposes of the not very detailed forms of the time, my step-father acted as my father. He was my safeguard.

I went to war none the less, via the normal recruitment office, but disguising the shameful details of my life – although even a prisoner's son would have been accepted as tenth-rate cannon-fodder. A year later, I was invalided out with severe shell-shock, and worked until the end of the war as a war correspondent for a peaceful little newspaper, which was entitled to employ low-ranking columnists. I had learnt from bitter experience not to complicate my application forms, and was haunted ever afterwards by the fear of being discovered.

It happened at the beginning of June, 1944. I made my routine trip to the front, saw that war was killing as many people as ever, became strangely depressed, and resolved to marry. I had been having an affair with a lovely young woman for almost a year, and we became man and wife. I moved into her house, which I discovered was very large and embarrassingly prosperous for those lean times. Everything was above-board, though; my father-in-law had some important job in industry.

The family enthusiastically celebrated each military success with a magnificent spread, and one evening we were drinking to the liberation of some town, I don't remember which, when the phone rang and Mama's unsmiling voice said: 'Come over!'

Nothing more was said, but I realized that my brief holiday was at an end, and that life had us again by the short hairs.

'Drinking again?' Mother asked as usual as I stepped through the door.

'Don't exaggerate.'

She handed me a telegram. Tomorrow at 6.10 a.m. we were to be at the Central Telegraph Office to take a call from Rokhma.

'Where's Rokhma?' I asked, surprised.

'You sound just like Mitya!' said Mother. 'Tell him someone's been run over by a tram, and he'll ask which street it was!'

My head suddenly cleared.

'Papa! Of course! My God!'

'Didn't you realize?' Mother said irritably.

'Why are you so angry?'

'I'm not angry, I'm just wondering how you can be like that, you poor man.'

But I understood. We were no longer playing for peanuts. How would my new family react to their unexpected alliance with an enemy of the people? The blameless life I had so carefully constructed for myself collapsed like a house of cards.

'To hell with it!' I cried, in a fit of depression and anger. 'I'm not betraying Father for those caviare-eaters!'

'Don't be so silly,' said Mother, who hated all affectation, however veiled. 'We'll do everything we possibly can for Mitya, but he doesn't exist. Do you understand? And no sentimentality. Not a word of this to Nina or any other girl, drunk or sober. Do you understand, Sergei? And now off to bed with you. You smell like a brewery.'

I went to bed, mortified by Mother's hardness and lack of emotion, and the cold, flat pragmatism with which she had greeted Father's resurrection. Yet buried in some little-noticed corner of my consciousness there glimmered a different and true version of what was happening: Mother had assumed responsibility for taking the harsh but necessary decisions. She was taking this weight off my shoulders and defending me from all the tormenting, shameful, dirty things I would have had to deal with had she not made the decision for me. The reason she was so serious and severe, so short on words and feelings, was that she was defending me both from myself and from life. She knew

I would be angry with her, and she let me play this pathetic game because she was stronger and more resilient than I.

At half-past five the following morning, we set off on foot for the Central Telegraph Office. It was a warm early June day, with clear white clouds in a clear blue sky, and utter silence in the empty, still sleeping streets. On just such a morning, at this time of year, Mama and I had set off seven years ago for Egorevsk to rediscover my father, just as we were doing now. The clipped grass on the wide streets was as green as the glades outside Moscow, and the lime trees on the Gogol and Suvorov Boulevards were as fragrant as the sweet smell that had flooded the open window of the railway carriage where Mama and I had sat, alone against the whole world.

Many terrible, irreparable things had happened in those seven years, many tears had been shed and fears endured, but there were also great mercies, small, pathetic joys, immense tiredness, barely noticed amidst life's daily round and crippling reverses. Mother had changed, too. It didn't matter to her whether I had had a 'good war' or not. Her back was as bent as an old woman's, her shoulders were hunched, and although her face had kept its clear, fine profile, it had collapsed into lines, wrinkles and blotches.

'D'you remember, Mama?' I asked, forgetting that she couldn't read my mind.

'What d'you mean? Oh, our journey to Egorevsk?' she said with a little smile.

And the way she immediately guessed my thoughts betrayed all the agitation she was trying so carefully to conceal.

'What extraordinary vitality Mitya has!' she said tenderly, and she must have been thinking that I had inherited this vitality from him.

They called us at ten to seven.

'Rokhma on the line!' announced a deep, muffled female voice from somewhere up in the ceiling. 'Cubicle three! Speak now!'

We rushed into the cubicle. There was none of the usual distant rustling or roaring, or interruptions from the operator. There was just emptiness, and suddenly from out of this emptiness, from the other end of the world and a far remote past, a distant but infinitely familiar voice pierced my heart: 'Seryozha . . .!'

Next day, loaded with two suitcases, as on my journey to Pinozero before the war, I set off for Rokhma, a small town near Ivanovo, where Father, released early because of illness, had been sent to live.

14

A New Meeting

I was no longer the boy who had visited Father at the Polar Circle four years back. I had been psychologically purified in battle; I had learnt to defend myself from enemy fire, if need be, and to direct my own bullet against myself – as had in fact happened while I was ill. Above all, I knew fear in all its aspects and nuances, and had developed such an instinct for danger that within certain limits I could maintain both my inner freedom and an almost equal lack of fear. I was already a full-grown man, in other words, in the sense that I had lost my emotional naïvety. But there was still a lot of the child in me.

For my journey to the godforsaken hole of Rokhma to visit my sick, suffering father, I was dressed up like a peacock. The reason for this inappropriate ostentation, I hazily explained to Mother, was my desire to impress the people of Rokhma, and thereby to raise Father's status there. But I don't think she believed me. What had really forced me into this foppery was the romantic, theatrical image I had of our meeting. Unfortunately I couldn't unfurl my scarlet sails, like Captain Grey, I couldn't arrive either in shining cuirasses, like Lohengrin, or even in the white tights and satin camisole of the prince-liberator in the ballet. So instead I went in a suit from Smirnov's, the best tailor in Moscow, with a wide gabardine cloak, a fashionable round cap and shoes with thick rubber soles. Elegant, handsome and rich, war veteran, son-in-law of a Moscow magnate, and a writer with a certain reputation to boot – this was how I would present myself to my old father. I would shower him with the good things of life, stowed away in my two suitcases. I would breathe new life into him, and inspire him to believe that with my support he would never fail.

Along with all this spiritual dross I did feel genuine warmth, and the joy of meeting, and tenderness, and pity. But all these feelings were somewhat abstract. As before, I was unable to imagine my father in the flesh; he was still the same for me as when I had last seen him, saddened by our parting, but none the less cheerful, strong and fit, with grey hair and a dark, youthfully attractive face. I knew quite well that he would no longer be the same, and that people let out of the camp early had already had all the life squeezed out of them and were good for nothing. But I simply couldn't amend my image of him accordingly. He had asked me to get him 'trousers, and if possible some footwear'. He asked me to bring him some 'bread and fats' – not butter, 'fats'. This must mean that he was utterly destitute and malnourished. Yet it didn't help to make my picture of him any clearer, on the contrary it grew even hazier, and dissolved. It was so much easier and pleasanter to imagine our exalted meeting, at which Father appeared in the image of the handsome, grey-haired old sufferer.

I was so intoxicated by the role awaiting me that as I changed trains in Ivanovo I carried my two heavy cases as easily as if they were filled with feathers. And a little over an hour later, when I clambered down on to the little Rokhma platform and discovered that the town was two miles away, it didn't bother me in the least, and hoisting a suitcase on to each shoulder, I stepped out boldly along the cobbled highway. I had covered half a mile or so when an empty cart drew up beside me and the driver offered me a lift. Since it wouldn't have done for a fairy-tale prince to arrive on a cart, I merely put my cases in. It was only then that I realized what a colossal weight I had been carrying on my shoulders. It still seems incredible that I could have walked half a mile dragging those cases, which together must have weighed a good ten stone.

I walked briskly beside the cart, past a sweet-smelling forest of fir trees, then past open fields and sky, until the high tower and red factory chimneys of a little town came into view.

Why did I single out that tiny far-off black dot at the side of the road? Why did I start peering at it more and more closely? Why, when the dot took on the vague, barely perceptible shape of a human form, did I pale and walk faster, overtaking the cart? On the way I had run into quite a few passers-by: men, women and children. Was it an instinctive memory of the time I had last seen him and he had lingered on in my vision, first as a speck, then as a black dot between the strands of the barbed wire? Now the same thing was happening in reverse – first a dot, then a figure – but I recognized Father the moment he appeared.

The driver whipped the horse, the cart drew level with me, and I quickened my step, trying to put some distance between us to help Father focus on me. I could see that the man tottering along the road was craning his neck and struggling to see me from such a long way off. Then he recognized me, or rather guessed it was me – his old eyes were no longer up to scanning such a distance – and started hobbling more quickly, clutching at his heart. I saw this gesture, and his strange shuffling gait, feebly dragging himself along, barely able to lift his feet off the ground.

'Papa!' I yelled, rushing towards him.

He stopped suddenly, as though unable to believe his eyes, and in the rush I noticed the incomprehensible expression of savage apprehension and estrangement on his shrivelled, cadaverous little face, with its thin, lumpy jaw.

'Papa!' I shouted again.

'Seryozha?' he said uncertainly.

We embraced. I couldn't kiss him properly – there was nowhere on his face to kiss. His thin mouth had disappeared into his cheeks and his upper lip. The flesh had fallen away from his face, leaving just the yellow skin covering the bones of his forehead, his cheekbones, his jaws, his nose and the boney lumps around his ears, such as one sees on people dying of starvation.

'I came out to meet you,' he said shyly, 'but I couldn't manage it . . .'

He bent down and started doing something to one of his shoes. What shoes! They were cut from an old car tyre, sewn together with something like a vein, and laced up with bits of string. His trousers were made of sack-cloth, with two matching blue patches on the knees. He wore a sort of shirt or overall, belted with string, which had once been black but had been bleached through repeated washing, and on his head he wore a ragged old flat cap.

The cart rumbled up beside us and stopped. I saw the surprised look on the driver's face.

'Get in,' I said to Father. 'He'll take us.'

'Hop in, hop in,' said the driver kindly, obviously realizing something.

Father went up to the cart, grappled with the back, then gave up.

'It's not far, let's walk . . .'

He hadn't the strength to get in.

'No, let's get in, I'll help you.'

I bent down, picked him up and put him in the cart. Of all the terrible experiences of that day, the most terrible was my feeling of disgust in that brief moment when I held Father in my arms. I had once had a similar experience. Some friends of mine had a

Japanese cat, an enormous creature with thick fluffy fur, which took up the whole of a large leather armchair. When I picked it up, however, it was almost weightless, and I found this disparity between its size and weight quite repulsive. The very word 'Father' is endowed with a certain weight and substance, but what I had lifted into the cart was without substance: I had made contact with something, but it had weighed less even than a child or a doll; there was not an ounce of human flesh beneath the sack-cloth trousers and bleached overall.

There were some desires still glimmering in this silent, fleshless creature, though. I felt a shiver on my back, and turning round, I saw a dirty little bag laid out on his sack-cloth knees, stuffed with what looked like sawdust, and some evenly cut squares of newspaper. I took out a packet of Kazbeks.

'Throw that rubbish away and have these,' I said.

I clicked the lighter, and on his noisy outbreath a fragrant blue cloud drifted from the cart. Something changed in the motionless bone mask; it was severed by little lines around the eyes and mouth, the thin seam of the mouth parted imperceptibly to reveal a single yellow incisor, and I didn't immediately realize that this feeble, agonized grimace was a smile of pleasure. And then I felt a touch, or rather the shadow of a touch, on my knee. I looked down, and saw a blotchy yellow object creep slowly up my leg, shyly caressing it. Bones covered with a dark blackish-yellow web, a frog's claw – and this claw, my God, was my father's hand.

15

Pellagra

Father lived in a little house on the town's main, oddly named Zamenhof Square. I thought this Zamenhof must have been some local hero who had raised the banner of revolution over Rokhma, but he turned out to be one of the founders of the lifeless language of Esperanto. It is still a mystery to me what connection the founder of Esperanto had with Rokhma, and why the town found it necessary to give his name to its main square, with its tower. It was just one of the perversions of this twisted, hideous little town, in which Father was to live out the rest of his days.

His quarters, a narrow little summer room, put me in mind of the plywood guard-house at the camp which had very nearly become our icy grave, and what I did the moment we got there was like a repeat of that distant episode. Opening my cases, I started loading the table with tins of stew, sausage, fish and condensed milk, meat, sugar, hunks of bread, cheese and ham, as well as a suit, shirts, socks, ties and shoes. Father watched me with silent concentration, asking no questions, indifferent to everything but the nutrition of which his body was so deprived. Picking up a slice from a two-pound packet of creamery butter, he started eating it without bread.

'Why don't you change,' I said, 'then we can eat.'

'Eat, eat . . .' he replied, like an echo.

Still holding the piece of butter in his hands, he scooped the clothes off the table and went to a corner to change, while I went to his landlady's rooms to ask her to heat up the samovar. She was sitting on the bed scratching a lifeless blue leg, an elderly, dishevelled woman with a puffy face and a wet, sagging lower lip. She made no answer to my request, but scratched on, leaving white stripes on her flesh that quickly turned red.

'Make some for yourself, too,' I hazarded, holding out the packet of tea and the blue-wrapped sugar lumps. She immediately stopped scratching and rose heavily from the bed.

Father was already changed when I returned to his room. But he looked no better in his new clothes, and his smart blue suit, shirt, tie and yellow Oxford shoes seemed merely to emphasize his pitiful thinness. He poured some sugar into his palm and put it in his mouth, casting baleful, sidelong glances at the tin of condensed milk. I got out a tin-opener and opened it. A few rich, sweet drops of milk fell on to the floor. He scooped them up with his fingers and licked them, and a few lines appeared in the corners of his eyes and mouth as that strange smile passed over his face again.

'What delicious stuff,' he said.

I gave him a teaspoon and, sitting down at the table with a look of solemn concentration, he dipped his spoon into the condensed milk.

'It's pellagra,' he said suddenly, after the fourth or fifth spoonful, carefully pushing the tin aside. He got up from the table and wandered over to the window.

I thought he was about to speak to me or ask me something, but instead he turned round, went back to the tin with a serious, even gloomy expression on his face, and ate another spoonful. And another, slowly, thoughtfully savouring this forgotten substance with all the senses in his body, while his brain tried to assimilate the heavenly, life-giving miracle contained in the thick, sugary concentration of milk.

The landlady brought in the cups and the samovar and hung

about the table, returning to her own room only after I had given her a white roll and a piece of sausage. Father drank no tea – he evidently had no need for liquids – but attacked the butter, cheese and sausage with renewed energy. However, the condensed milk wouldn't leave him alone. He kept dipping in his spoon and taking just one more mouthful. He even flirted with the tin, picking it up with a proprietorial air and slowly scraping the sides with his spoon, or creeping up on it like a thief and stealing one more precious drop, or carelessly plunging his spoon into the yellow density and scooping out a brimming spoonful.

'You'll be ill,' I said.

'I know,' he replied, putting down his spoon.

But a moment later I saw him furtively dipping his finger in the tin again and licking it.

It saddened and depressed me to see my father, always so frugal and fastidious, reduced to this state of physical degradation. He did soon become ill, of course, for his poor, unused stomach was unable to keep the food down. He managed to reach the yard to throw up. He came back, ate a little more, and retched again. Then he had diarrhoea. Poor Father staggered from his room to the boarded coop standing amidst the tall burdocks at the bottom of the yard, then struggled back again, growing steadily weaker and weaker. Yet he still couldn't stop nibbling little mouthfuls of food and spoonfuls of condensed milk. The terrible idea suddenly came to me that I was helping to kill him, but I was unable to do anything about it, and hadn't the heart to take the food from him.

As he came back into the room, a strange 'Poof, poof' sound, like bursting bubbles, issued from his sunken cheeks. I wondered if he had heartburn. 'Have some soda water,' I suggested.

'No,' he said, smiling his weak and now slightly crafty smile, 'I think I'll just have another spoonful of that condensed milk.'

As he went to the table, his trousers fell down – he evidently hadn't the strength to do them up properly – and I saw his tiny stick legs, and his huge round cannon-ball knees. Suddenly I could no longer separate myself from him – he and I were one flesh. I felt all his frailty, his powerlessness, his suffering and his pain, I felt the shakiness of his spindly shins, the weight of his boney cannon-ball knees, the insatiable hunger sucking at his empty body. It made me feel queasy. I couldn't stay in that room. I needed to find some relief, some secure, sober normality. All my healthy appetites and instincts rebelled against this morbid hypnosis which drugged one's brain and soul. Fortunately Father came to my rescue.

'I'll have a little sleep now,' he said, collapsing on to the bed.

'Well, I've got some things to do,' I responded. 'I came here on an assignment, it was the only way I could get a ticket. I'll go to the district committee office, and then to the factory to meet the planners . . .'

I was speaking into the void – Father was already asleep, his mouth gaping open like a corpse.

Not one of my journalistic assignments have I carried out with such relish and enthusiasm as this one, which I could easily have disregarded, since my editors knew I was on compassionate leave. I had never been so pleased to enter a district secretary's office. I loved the inevitable conference table with its red calico cloth covered in pearly ink-stains, I loved the dusty curtains in the windows, the portraits on the wall, and the secretary himself, looking like district secretaries throughout the length and breadth of the country, with his short buttoned-up field-jacket and matching trousers tucked into boots.

The district committee rescued me from what was happening

with Father; I was rescued by the flax-spinning combine, where I went with the secretary, by gossip about the output planners, by the up-to-date day nurseries, the Board of Honour, the Stakhanovite shock-workers, the innovative director, and finally the canteen, where the secretary and the director vied with each other to ply their Moscow guest with food.

I returned, feeling somewhat revived, to the little house on Zamenhof Square, to find Father polishing off the remains of the condensed milk, scraping the metal sides of the tin with his spoon.

'How do you feel?' I asked him.

'Better, I think.' He listened to what was going on inside him, and repeated, 'Better.'

Encouraged by this, I started telling him about my outing: about my welcome at the district office and the flax combine, about all the material I'd collected and about my excellent lunch at the managers' canteen. There was a hidden subtext to all this. Father had always had a most respectful attitude to those in power, and I thought it would give him confidence to hear about my friendship with the Rokhma high-ups. But he paid no attention to my story. He had in front of him everything he needed from me: butter, condensed milk and endless tins. Only once did a flicker of interest appear on his face, when I told him about the canteen.

'So you've already had lunch,' he said pensively, 'And I'd just asked our landlady to put on some potatoes.'

It was still light when we went to bed. I smoked one cigarette after another, unable to sleep. I had just dropped off when the half moon flooded the window with green light and banished sleep. The moon turned the white walls of the room green, covering the floor with the angular shadow of the window transom and turning the pile of uncleared foods on the table into something dark and mysterious. Then Father, who had been sleeping as quietly as a mouse, rolled his head on the pillow, gave a little groan, got up, green-faced as a mermaid, and walked with outstretched arms to the table, groped for a bit of food and started chewing. Then shuffling slowly back to bed, he gave a deep, childlike sigh and lay down. Several more times in the course of that sleepless night I saw spasms of uncontroll-able hunger break his sleep and force him to make that journey from the bed to the table.

16

The Blue Tree

When I woke next morning I sensed at once that something had changed. Father was sitting on his bed smoking, his face half turned towards me, and I saw one limpid, lively dark brown eye peering at me with affectionate curiosity. Yesterday's evil spell had passed; tortured, sick and devoured by hunger, my father had come back to me.

He was terribly weak, the sight of food still enticed and tormented him, and at times he fell into a sort of hunger-induced faint, yet it was clear that his experiences had not only failed to destroy him, but that they had left his spirit intact; a prudent compliance, yes, but not a trace of resentment, resignation or servile meekness, and still with all his old good-natured interest in life and people, still as ready as ever for a joke – he called Rokhma the 'last lark of a lifetime'. He spoke calmly, simply and very sparingly about what had happened to him, without anger or self-pity, and without spinning out his own sufferings. Later I understood that only the weak talked willingly about the brutal violence to which they were subjected in the camps. Those who still had their pride would never admit to having been tortured, beaten and tormented. They would rather whitewash their tormentors than expose their own trampled human dignity. Having drunk his full measure of camp life, and lived through all the cruelty of the war panic, Father had of course had some experience of fear and humiliation. But only once, very unwillingly, did he admit that the soldier escorting him on some journey had struck him with his rifle-butt. I think he told Mother more, but me he tried to spare; I was young, I had my life to live, and I didn't need to know how they could beat someone's soul out of him.

He was like a diamond, which can be scratched only by another diamond, but which resists even the crudest, most powerful tools of iron and steel. I wasn't a diamond, I belonged to that unlucky, impure generation born after the Revolution; honest within limits, steadfast within limits, good within limits – in other words, able in a crisis to choose between death and betrayal. For Father no such choice existed; for him there was only death. This is what made him so incorruptible and so emotionally defenceless. This debilitated little man in the falling-down trousers had the purity, fortitude and spirit of a Lohengrin, and beneath the velvet, feathers and cuirasses of his deliverer lurked a Telramund. And I had come to inspire him with fortitude, courage and the power to live! The whole of that morning before I left he poured into me this good, life-giving power, which is possibly the greatest of all blessings: the capacity to live without hardening one's heart, to respect the joy of existence, to go forward without leaving shreds of one's soul on the thorns of life, like a mangy dog leaving clumps of fur on the burdocks.

He didn't talk about these things in a lecturing way, of course – Father never spoke to me in a didactic tone, merely as an older man talking to a younger one – yet we might as well have had a long discussion about it. He also sensed, with his usual extraordinary sensitivity to those he loved, that I was not as grand as I would have liked to be. He sensed prince, and he wanted to help me to become one.

'You know,' he said, pointing to my right temple, 'there's something heroic about that.'

I was stunned by his perceptiveness. Every young man derives confidence from some particular aspect of his appearance. It's usually something crudely obvious, like a moustache or sideboards, or a particular way of doing one's hair or holding one's head. There was nothing really very remarkable about this right temple of mine, its smoothly brushed-back hair lightly scattered with grey. But when I looked at myself in the mirror in private, I would focus on this temple, and I would fancy that it swept my face upwards, free of its normal gross heaviness. To understand this, however, Father had had to be me for a moment. He *could* be me, and I could be him . . .

I left later that day, and he came to see me off. We walked slowly across the square towards the cobbled highway running from the town to the station. After two or three steps he clutched his heart and stopped to catch his breath. In the half-hour it took us to cross Zamenhof Square – with its blank, unfriendly little houses and ridiculous pink tower, the wooden gates and plywood ticket-offices of the park, the impoverished stalls and the solemn spiteful geese and dirty mangy pigs jostling for the pond, which was as big as the square itself – I got to know the place so well that I shall hate it for the rest of my life.

At last the tower fell off to our right, and the highway sprang up in front of us, bright with colour after the recent rain. A line of telegraph poles disappeared into the distance, above the fresh green of the fields a city of clouds piled up their domes, towers and spires on the edge of the clear blue sky, and the air was filled with the poignant fresh smell of earth and washed grass. Either this superabundance of freshness took Father's breath away, or the imminent parting had put a strain on his heart, for he paused for a long time, hanging his head, breathing heavily and wheezily through his nose.

'You don't have to come with me,' I said. 'Go back home, or I'll worry about you.'

'No, no,' he replied in a firm, serious voice. 'Let's go.'

We walked on, so slowly that the pedestrians overtaking us kept looking back at us in amazement. After several paces, Father had another attack. His face pale, his eyes staring, he stood clasping his chest, as though trying to catch his slipping heart.

'No, no,' he said, forestalling my shy protest. 'We must go on. We must go on as far as that telegraph pole.' And there was such an uncharacteristic determination in his voice that I said nothing.

Father was not known to be particularly stubborn or superstitious, nor did he play anxious guessing games, but now for some reason he had to walk as far as that post, to make this short and agonizing journey without giving in, even if it destroyed his heart. Maybe he was setting himself some important personal test; maybe he wanted to discover some secret reserve of strength without which he wouldn't survive until our next meeting. Beating back weariness, he rose above his infirmity and walked on.

One post gone, and another. Fearing to look at him, I involuntarily quickened my step, as though it were up to me to reach that post. But this seemed to help him, as though I were pulling him along like an invisible tug. Refusing my help, almost collapsing at every step, he bent forwards, overtook me and stretched out his hand to the post, then pressed his whole body against it. I put my palm beside his on its warm wet circumference, inaudibly vibrating like a live thing. We looked at each other: something important had happened, some victory, although over what or whom I didn't know.

'Well, it's over,' said Father. 'And I survived.' He looked at me with a strange smile, and added: 'I chose this place myself, you see. No one ordered me to.'

We stood there silently for a while. Before us, rising above the side of the forest where the road was, I saw the dense bushy top of a tree. It might have been an oak, an elm or an old weeping willow, it was impossible to tell from that distance. Its thick leafy crown looked blue above the jagged bright green wall of the fir forest, and was severed by a thread of steam, the evaporation from the recent rain, so that the top seemed to be hanging freely in the air.

'I'll come back in a month,' I said to Father, 'and we'll walk as far as that tree together.'

I walked quickly to the station along the hard, well-trodden path which wound beside the highway. The blue tree hung above the forest, and it seemed at first to be quite near, on the very edge of the wood. Then it moved back into the depths of the forest, and when I stepped into the resinous fragrance of the wet, sun-warmed fir grove, it jumped back again and re-appeared beyond the tracks of the railway line. But when I reached the tracks, the blue tree hid behind a sparse thicket of aspens. Its light powerful dome towered above the fine trembling tops of the aspens, and I realized that Father and I would never reach that tree – the blue tree of joy.

17

Under Rokhma Skies

There was no joy, to be sure – how could there be! But life went on with the occasional ray of hope, and many more of grief and hardship. True, the next time I arrived in Rokhma – exactly a month later – it was with a proud and happy feeling. I was greeted on Zamenhof Square by a small, thin, even dapper gentleman, dressed respectably, even foppishly by Rokhma standards, with a lively smile and brisk gestures but a terribly slow step. Father looked better fed, he had put some flesh on his bones, he had new teeth and had lost the ghastly hollows under his cheeks, although his heart had been damaged beyond repair. But there remained even in this newly restored self of his that amazing appetite for life which had so delighted Mama.

He was now lodging with a different landlady, not far from the Great Rokhma textile mill, where he had found work as a planner. His former landlady was not satisfied with the rather high rent he had agreed by previous arrangement to pay her, so he had had to move. He subsequently had to make several more changes of address. The moment his landladies found out that he had some money, their mouths would water. They would rather lose a quiet, reliable lodger than live with the idea, heaven forbid, that he wasn't paying them enough. This was typical of the stiflingly greedy kulak mentality of the citizens of Rokhma.

This little town, with its two textile mills, might have been considered a working town but for the fact that there were virtually no real workers in it. There were some tiny smallholdings, run by people who had served their term of labour conscription and were thus entitled to own a vegetable patch, some pigs, some chickens and a cow, to use the pastures around the town and to engage in a little speculation in nearby Ivanovo. These were the indigenous inhabitants of the town. Apart from them, working in the Great Rokhma Mill and the flax combine were newcomers: drunken, promiscuous, unhappy women mobilized God knows from where or by whom, and some war invalids who had been classed as fit to work in the rear. These people huddled together in the barracks and didn't belong to the town. Its real face was created in the image of Father's landladies: malicious, dim-witted, and so greedy that it often worked against their interests.

People didn't like Father there. Neither his inoffensiveness, nor his weakness, nor his equable, cheerful nature were any defence against their hatred. They hated him for having been in a camp and for having got out, for not dying of hunger and going around barefoot and in rags, for having a son who was a writer, and for the fact that this son had not abandoned him in his misfortune. However, I only had to send him his money a few days late once to get an anonymous letter threatening to report me to the Union of Writers for not helping my old father. The unknown writer of this letter was prompted less by the desire to do Father a good turn than to get back at me for helping him.

During my second visit to Rokhma, I remember, I accompanied him to the factory. They were doing the accounts, and he had to give up half his free day to work on them. As before in the camp, I followed him to his desk, meeting his colleagues in the office, shaking their hands, being told their names and telling them mine; then I watched him work, and heard the forgotten rattle of the arithmometer and the resounding click of the abacus beads. Everything was the same as it had been long ago, yet everything was different. I didn't catch one smile or one kind or interested glance from these people, or any responsive warmth in their handshakes. They looked at me with sullen suspicion, sticking out their limp, sweaty hands, and immediately snatching them back again, and the only question they asked me was about the prices in Moscow's markets. Father now worked with none of his old élan. He had to check his figures several times, got angry with the arithmometer, furrowed his brow in annoyance, having lost some figure, crossed something out and started all over again. His constricted blood vessels were evidently not sending enough hot, live blood to his brain.

He was the only one of them working, too. His boss, Sharov, twice left the building for a long time to unload some cotton. There were not enough loaders, and they were roping in the workers from the office, but it was such hard, dirty work, and the pay was so miserable – a pound of black bread and a few worthless roubles – that no one but Sharov would do it. Sharov was the oldest worker there and the wealthiest man in town, with a large dairy farm, butter churns, a cheese dairy and some greenhouses and orchards. But he was such a perfect example of the Rokhma mentality that he would have taken on any job for a few extra copecks.

Another of Father's colleagues in the office kept running off to feed her baby; the third, who barely appeared, had got leave to do some business in Ivanovo; the fourth was permanently drunk and either slept or noisily and hopelessly swigged water from a carafe; and the fifth, a solemn, youthful-looking man, leafed through the newspapers for a while, went out for a smoke, came back and shuffled things about on his desk, then left again for another smoke.

The only time these sluggish, somnolent people showed any interest was when Father was to blame for a sharp exchange in the office. My camp-crippled Father was not only a much more conscientious worker than the others, he was also more flippant, which was his way of trying to protect his own identity. It happened like this: the nursing mother, a plump, large-breasted, flat-bottomed woman with a secretive, suspicious Rokhma face locked and bolted shut, complained that her house was being overrun by rats.

'We used to eat rats in the camp,' remarked Father, tearing himself away from his arithmometer.

There was an ominous silence – not of sleep, but of awakening. His words had released the kingdom of sleep from its spell, like the prince's kiss awakening the court of the Sleeping Beauty, only this produced not activity but the tense stillness of hounds about to pounce.

The youthful-looking man stopped fiddling with his next cigar. The drunkard took the carafe from his mouth. The nursing mother slid one more bolt shut on her closed face.

But these good people were then terrified by their own silence. The youthful-looking man moved his chair, signifying both a protest and a readiness to take action. The drunkard grunted. And the mother, speaking not only for herself but for her defenceless offspring, said in a stiff, frightened voice:

'What on earth did you do that for?'

'Why, so as to keep the rodents down, of course,' Father said lightly.

It's not hard to imagine how this conversation might have ended, had not Sharov suddenly returned from unloading cotton and helped Father out.

'Don't ask stupid questions!' he said sharply to the woman. 'You're not a baby!'

At this everyone immediately lost interest in the subject. The woman was employed in the office thanks only to Sharov, as were the other two; none of them were good for anything, in fact, and one word from Sharov could have lost them their jobs.

Sharov defended Father partly because he valued him as a worker, and partly because for all his greed he was an honest man. He was convinced in his heart of hearts that Father had merited his sentence, however, and kulak that he was, he couldn't help sympathizing with him. He showed his kindness to us by inviting us to visit him. We went that evening, admired his model farm, his beautiful apple and cherry orchards, his blackcurrants and his pollen-covered gooseberries; we watched his eldest daughter milking the magnificent red Kostroma cow, the middle one briskly churning the butter, and the youngest busily feeding the pigs, chickens, ducks and geese. Then Sharov whispered something to his old wife, and we saw her pull a large silver samovar into the passage, while the eldest daughter brought out an earthenware pot of thick cream and a bowl of honey, swimming with transparent bees' wings. But we never got our refreshments, for Sharov evidently had second thoughts about sharing it with us. So, taking our leave of our hospitable hosts, we made our way back to Father's room through the night streets of Rokhma, which were every bit as unfriendly, unattractive and unpoetic as those of daytime Rokhma.

18

Friends and Relations

In the years that followed I made several more visits to Rokhma, and each new visit became more painful for me. I not only failed to get used to my double life, I found it increasingly shameful and agonizing. In the train I would be clad in my Moscow armour, but the moment the familiar tower and the red chimneys of the Great Rokhma Mill loomed into sight, I would shed not only my armour but my skin. I felt naked and vulnerable, and was utterly humiliated by this descent from the palace to the mud.

The insecurity of my split existence at that time induced a permanent premonition of the ultimate, shameful calamity of discovery. At times I felt tempted to be done with it, to reveal my Rokhma secret and start afresh in a new, humbler but more honourable life. But I had no right to do this: it would have spelt the end not just for me but for Father, for I was the well-spring of his existence.

Lacking the strength to be consistent, I only partly acted on Mama's decision. As far as my closest friends in Moscow were concerned, my prisoner father did not exist. I hadn't the heart to tell him this, though. He would sing my praises throughout Rokhma with reckless indiscretion, and I lived in dread of some Rokhma itinerant knocking at my regal father-in-law's door in search of a room or a job. I felt like a thief, waiting for someone to grab my collar.

I was also unspeakably oppressed by the hopelessness of Father's situation. It was a drama without the salutary purification of catharsis. I could no longer dream, as I once did, of that moving, triumphant day when Father would throw off his chains, emerge into the light and return home to Moscow to end his days in happiness. I should never be able to take him by the arm and lead him proudly down the street. Between me and this dream stood an impregnable wall of lies – my entire new biography, pages of personal records, as light and as burdensome as my life itself. In expunging Father from my biography, I was expunging him from the dream which ever since my adolescence, and even my childhood, had represented the supreme, ultimate meaning of my life. Nothing will ever make amends for this, neither his cruel and senseless sufferings, nor our tears. His heroic resilience, courage and forbearance were all useless. The blue tree of joy was a mere chimera.

At the time I am describing, there was still a lot that Father didn't know, although he must have had an inkling of what was going on. It wasn't fear that blinded him to our ordeal – he had spent years being ruled by fear – so he had never sunk to the kind of loss of personality or the treacherous, life-saving sophistry that would have enabled him to straddle the gap between heroism and banality. He was very naïve, and he paid cruelly for his naïvety.

This is what happened in the first years after the war, when they had just restored the telephone line between Rokhma and Moscow.

He entered the warm little building of the telephone exchange, where the girl behind the barrier, her eyes bleary from lack of sleep, was irritably stabbing the brass tips of the wires into the switchboards. She put so much angry energy into what she was doing that it looked as though she wanted to skewer right through the board.

Father had thought that today he would be in luck, but now

all hope abandoned him. He stood behind the barrier, not daring to speak. This was the fourth time he had come. It had taken him a long time to screw up the courage to telephone. One call would cost him twenty-five roubles – the price of a jug of milk, two pounds of potatoes, or a pound of bread. But finally he couldn't bear it any longer, and his longing to hear a friendly voice overcame the reawakened pangs of hunger. He had come three times to no avail. That meant getting up at five in the morning. Waking was murder: sleep was his one blessed release from loneliness and the insistent agony of his restored and ravenous body.

As always, he awoke to see his room filled with the furniture of his childhood, congealed by dense clots of shadow. The sideboard, huge as a castle – when he was a child it *was* a castle, which he had often stormed with his brother, who was now dead; and behind the sideboard the wardrobe, and the nurse's iron-studded trunk, and the two horned bicycles leaning against the wall, and the two writing desks, the bigger one his brother's the smaller one his. He could see it all, he could undeniably see it – he just had to stretch out his hand and he'd touch his childhood things. But he never did so after his first disappointment, and he waited instead for the things to disappear by themselves, melting away with the first light filtering through the thin shutter. And that is what happened: the wardrobe would disappear, then the desks, then the bicycles, and the sideboard would stay the longest. First its base would dissolve, leaving the carved top of its middle turret suspended under the ceiling, then that too would disappear, and nothing would remain but the walls of the empty room, containing just the bed and a bit of plywood on four legs that served as his table.

For so many years he had woken in these bare, unfurnished places: the wooden walls and bunks of the barracks; the logs of the hut, and a scrap of sky containing the Pole Star, as large and as close as a drop of milk; and lastly his bare rooms in Rokhma, from which his landladies would remove every scrap of furniture before letting them. So his cunning subconscious mind had played this consoling little game with him, filling his room with his childhood things. The first time he had thought this illusion was real and, getting up, he had gone towards them, stretched out his hand – and touched the rough bare wall. He never did it again, content with the small, brief joy of seeing them in the moments between sleeping and waking . . .

He went out into the street. Light was already creeping across the edge of the sky, and the tops of the old trees were starkly outlined against the horizon, but the ground was still in darkness, and everything on it seemed to blend together. He knew that by the time he reached the telephone exchange it would be completely light. He had worked out that to cover the three thousand steps separating him from us would take him an hour and a half, during which time nature's colours, sounds and climate would have changed.

He broke up his route into three stages: his first stopping-place was by the shop outside the entrance to the factory, the second was by the railings of the bridge over the river, and the last was on the bench outside the park. The hardest stage was the first, from the house to the factory. Here the road led almost imperceptibly uphill, and his heart reacted painfully to any physical exertion. He knew from the start that his heart would keep stopping, then pound furiously to push the sluggish blood along the delicate thread-like vessels. In order to survive, he had to learn not to hurry, not to step out like a soldier, but to take one step at a time, like a little child learning to go upstairs – slow and careful, that was the way, he'd get there in the end . . .

As he crossed the bridge, the dusk lifted, the violet-coloured effluent from the factories glinted with red, and the brick façade of the textile mill glowed as though enveloped in flames. As he reached the park, the darkness gathered around the foot of the trees and fences, and the air cleared.

Once again his heart started to pound painfully, not from the exertions of the journey this time, but with hope. He must just clutch his heart, empty his mind and try to look about him – at that cart loaded with silver pots, trundling to the market, or that peasant woman carrying a goose in a basket, sticking out its long neck, its foolish little head and huge red beak. And there ahead was the little telephone exchange; he'd made it, and it wouldn't be his last journey yet!

The girl, ignoring him, pulled the tips of the wires out of some sockets on the switchboard and stuck them into some others. Wrong one! Flicking her wrist with annoyance, she took out one tip and thrust it into the next socket. He felt envious of her rough, fretful movements, and the fact that she didn't have to conceal her irritation, or even notice that he was there.

'I wonder if I might trouble you,' he said at last. 'You promised me today . . .'

The brass tips jangled, reverberating against the aluminium switchboard, and the girl connected up some voices. One movement of her hand, and an invisible line of conversation unwound into the morning air. The ease with which she did this for people amazed him. He hadn't the strength to repeat his request. Then the girl herself said: 'Wait a minute. I've got the Great Mill on the line.'

He waited. A long time. He could imagine their conversation.

'How about unbleached cotton?'

'That should be OK.'

'Any problems?'

'A few problems.'

'And calico?'

'Calico's OK, too.'

'And tusser?'

'Tusser's OK.'

. . . The long jangling ring of the telephone pierced the family's morning sleep, like a signal of impending calamity. It woke everyone, yet no one could get up.

'What is it?' asked my wife in alarm.

'Probably one of our old relatives asking for money.'

'Then I wish she'd die,' sighed my wife, pulling the blanket over her head.

'Your Moscow call's not answering,' the operator said irritably.

'They must still be asleep . . . Would you be so good as to try once more . . .?'

The operator wound the handle of the receiver, and wound it again. The receiver filled with rustling, crackling sounds, like wind stirring along an autumn forest path; a thin drone, then a quiet, regular tapping, like rain drumming on the leaves; then a sort of distant music, swelling up, surging closer, then receding again and disppearing into the distance. The voice of space is plaintive and troubled, and fills the heart with fear. Then suddenly, from far, far away, at the other end of the world, he clearly heard the voice of his former wife:

'Yes?'

The tiny line had finally reached out to him, and tiny though it was, he suddenly felt terribly close to this long-lost family from which he was probably excluded now for ever.

'Hello there, Katya!' he yelled. 'How are you all?'

'All right.' The voice was stiff and cold – but maybe it was just the distance that made it sound so.

Clutching at the receiver as though afraid it might be snatched away from him, he shouted:

'And how's Seryozha?'

'All right.'

'Is he doing well?'

'All right.'

There was irritation in her voice. He knew that tone well from the far-off years when they had been married, but he hadn't expected to hear it now. His heart throbbed with a dull anxious ache. He couldn't ask why this was happening to him – for years he hadn't been able to ask why it was like that. He just thought of the long, hard road he'd had to walk to get here, and by which he would have to return.

Standing barefoot on the floor, his former wife distinctly heard the timidity and bewilderment in his voice, but what could she do? If it hadn't been so early she would have been quicker off the mark, but her drowsy brain couldn't take it in. Say something, anything . . .

'How are you feeling now?'

'There are only two things wrong with me: my heart, and a very healthy appetite,' joked Father from the other end of the world.

She sensed a faint note of hope in his voice.

'What can we do, things are hard for everyone,' she said – not at all what he'd been expecting, as she herself realized the moment she'd said it. She had meant to say that it wasn't her fault, but she hadn't been able to find the right words, and the line snapped . . .

What else *could* she have done? She couldn't even address him by name – their son had his wife staying, who must know nothing. Heaven forbid that she might guess.

19

The 'Closets'

The inordinate greed of Father's Rokhma landladies brought him to the 'Closets', a sort of workers' hostel beside the Great Rokhma Mill. The huge four-storey brick building of the 'Closets' had been constructed by one Kushchinsky, the former owner of the mill, and had clearly been conceived as some sort of liberal experiment.

Its high-ceilinged, large-windowed rooms opened on to wide, spacious corridors, running the entire length of the building. At the end of each corridor were vast communal kitchens and sitting-rooms, and on the ground floor were showers and laundries. The 'Closets', as Kushchinsky's commune was dubbed, was not a success. Workers longed for the land. The single ones achieved this by marrying a local woman, and families preferred to live in wretched cramped hovels with their own plot of land. As a result, the 'Closets' became the living-quarters for the dregs of the workforce – unmarried peasant women, boozers, prostitutes, in short the whole déclassé ragtag and bobtail of society. During the Revolution and the ensuing havoc, the crowd at the 'Closets' became even more mixed: vagrant men and women, armless and legless soldiers, and various 'divorcees' with their innumerable offspring. This dense human stew crammed the showers, the laundries and the communal sitting-rooms. Only the kitchen remained empty, since its huge stoves, unlit by the cheerful crackle of gas, offered no 'living space'.

Some rooms contained two or three families piled up on top of each other, in others the space was comfortably occupied by a single resident. All the rooms emitted the stale, pungent smells of cooking into the corridors, and primuses buzzed incessantly like huge bumblebees. Kushchinsky's kitchens had been unused since time immemorial; they had been built on the assumption of some communal basis to the inhabitants' lives, and this automatically made them unusable. Even the collective purchase of firewood seemed beyond these disconnected, suspicious people, who secretly and openly hated one another.

The native citizens of Rokhma heartily despised the inhabitants of the 'Closets'. To live there meant to go downhill, and to sink hopelessly in public esteem. This hardly troubled Father at all; what troubled him was the fact that he had no room of his own, however wretched, but had to rent a corner of one from a devout, middle-aged Suzdal 'divorcee', who worked at a local factory. When I visited Father in his new quarters, I realized that here at least no one would pester him by constantly raising his rent or board – a cold samovar in the morning and a bowl of cold porridge in the evening. Here danger was threatening him from another direction.

His landlady, whose pious face looked as though it was annointed in oil from the icon-lamp, regarded Father with her shining, voracious eyes as a mouse in a trap. Gliding silently about the room, or stepping out of her ample dress, she was perpetually rummaging about in the bed, the cupboard or the shelf, as though looking for something she had lost. All this was merely a ploy to enable her not to leave us alone. I don't know if she was afraid that I would set Father against her, or if she was excited by the presence of two men, but I sensed that things might turn out badly for my poor weak father who was so incapable of defending himself.

The woman finally volunteered to buy us some vodka – this

was the first time I had ever had a drink in Rokhma. We gave her some money and, wrapping herself up in a dingy woollen shawl, she hurled her restless body out into the corridor.

'Your landlady obviously has designs on you,' I said to Father.

'I'm afraid she has,' he agreed. 'She paces about at night in a white shroud of a nightdress, looking like death . . . I have a friend here,' he went on. 'She's called Fisa, a lovely woman – we'll go and see her later, I've been longing for you two to meet.'

'Tell me about her.'

'She's a weaver. Her husband died at the front, leaving her with two children, a boy and a girl. The boy is uncommonly slow – he's had to spend three years in every class. He'll be called up soon, and he's still in a class of twelve year olds. Her daughter's lively and quite clever, but she's a cunning little thing. She wanted to call me Papa, but I soon put a stop to that.'

'So I've got a new little brother and sister?'

'Oh, no!' Father reassured me with naïve solemnity. 'That will never happen. Fisa is an unselfish person, and wants nothing from me. People are always criticizing her for forming an attachment with an "old man", and not "getting anything out of it", as the local women put it. She is genuinely fond of me.'

'So why don't you move in with her? Anything would be better than the Closets.'

'Thereby hangs a tragic tale. Fisa lived with an old woman whom she fed and cared for, and in return the old woman was going to leave her the house after she died. The woman proved to be exceptionally tenacious, and she completely wore Fisa out. When eventually she died, we were so happy! I bought wine, Fisa baked cakes. Then about three weeks later I was spending the night with her and suddenly, terribly late, there was a knock at the door. Standing outside were two blind beggars, husband and wife, who were distant relatives of the old woman, and her legal heirs. Someone from Rokhma, envious of Fisa's good luck, had gone to the trouble of tracing these blind folk and telling them about their legacy. My heart almost broke with pity for her . . .'

'So what happened?'

'They spent the night on the floor, and when I woke next morning I heard a rustling sound: they were going over each other for lice, and crushing them between their teeth. It was disgusting,' Father said dispassionately. 'They then made an inventory of everything in the house, and discovered that the chimney of the samovar was damaged, so they went off to Penza to get a new one.'

'They went to Penza for that?'

'Blind people travel free on the trains, and they're better treated there than they are on the street. I can't imagine they'll stay here long,' he added thoughtfully. 'People hate beggars in Rokhma. The old man stood outside our factory all day, and he didn't even get the price of a tot of vodka.'

'But what if they sell the house?'

'No one'd want that rotting hovel! It'll be a matter of a hundred roubles at the most, and I'll be able to help Fisa out with that.' Father smiled. 'It's pleasant to become a property owner in one's declining years!'

His landlady returned with a small bottle of vodka, a bottle of beer and some things to eat. Staining the vodka with raspberry syrup, she briskly set the table, then retired to the corner, beneath the blackened silver frames of the icons, and leaning her head on her hand, she gazed tenderly at her feasting 'boyfriends'.

I had to go to the lavatory; it was at the end of the corridor,

Father said, on the left. Walking along the high, echoing corridor, I saw a row of little doors, half covered in opaque purple glass. Pushing one door, I found myself in someone's room: a jumble of walls and possessions, the deafening roar of a primus stove, the shrieking racket of children. A second attempt produced the same result. I didn't try to open any more doors, I merely had to put my ear to the dull purple glass to hear behind every door the noise of life. I walked on further and ended up in a great hall filled with the largest stoves I had ever seen – a real witches' kitchen! It was impossible to imagine simple human meals being cooked here. No, this must be where Satan used to do his fiery business, roasting sinners in frying pans as big as knights' shields. But now the mighty ships' boilers had fallen into disuse, and the stoves were as cold as burial vaults.

Gripped by a nervous chill, I quickly crossed the kitchen and pushed some door at random to find myself in another vast hall which differed little from the first. A cold grey tarpaulin-like material was glued to the floor, the walls and the ceiling, which oozed a loathsome greenish slime. The only dry spot in this dank, sweating place was a cobweb which smothered the tall gothic window from top to bottom. Sticking up in the middle of the hall, like an outlandish flower, were two cast-iron lavatory pans on one tubular stalk. There was no other furniture. On one of the walls someone had scrawled in excrement: 'Hitler is a pidorast.' The inscription was right under the ceiling, so whoever had written it would have had to stand on someone's shoulders to do so. The large clumsy letters stood out starkly against the greenish slime on the wall.

This cold, damp, sepulchral hall, with its cobweb-covered window, its cast-iron flower and its eloquent inscription under the ceiling, seemed like some sick dream, and to this day I sometimes wonder if it ever really existed.

When I returned to Father's room, he was standing by the window, staring out at the street, and from behind his shoulder I saw a funeral procession. Four emaciated horses, in dirty white funeral cloths and black blinkers, pulled along a hearse with a coffin inside. Both hearse and coffin were draped with red calico, on which were palely inscribed the letters of some slogans. Behind the coffin walked a cheerful crew of five or six musicians. Short, echoing notes issued from the glimmering snake of the euphonium, as battered as though it had been in a skirmish with the Archangel Michael, while four trumpets wove their own thin dirge into its murky voice. Two or three bars of Chopin's Funeral March would occasionally break through this chaos of sound. Following the musicians walked two men in mourning coats, clumsily dragging a huge tin wreath, and straggling behind them for a quarter of a mile were the mourners. The further they were from the bier, the more disorderly their ranks and the more apathetic their faces, and bringing up the rear were brawny girls, arm in arm as though at a demonstration.

'When I die,' said Father, 'please let me be buried without music. This is my one, solemn request. The musicians are hired from the park band, and they're continually breaking into the Foxtrot. I shan't take any pleasure from my death if I can't be sure that they won't accompany me to my grave.'

. . . Poor Father! He needn't have bothered, for it happened just as he had feared it would, and the gang from the park band, breaking from Chopin's Funeral March into the Foxtrot, accompanied him on his last journey. Such was Fisa's inflexible will. Her acquaintance with Father had brought a moment of brightness and joy to her life, and she couldn't refuse him this final honour – people would never forgive her . . .

This visit broke something in me. Our room was a wretched

little cell in the stone honeycomb of the monstrous hostel, teaming with hatred, poverty, filth and violence. Nothing but flimsy, fragile partitions separated us from terrible people who dreamed up cast-iron lavatories and smeared walls with excrement. From this helplessness it seemed but a step to the coffin, dragged by half-blind nags. Never had Father sunk to such misery!

I sent our landlady out for more vodka, and poured myself glass after glass without even getting drunk. The landlady dashed out again and again, glad to be of service to her 'boyfriend'. A girl with a soft, sweet face and dirty painted fingernails appeared from somewhere, drank some vodka, took my hand and stroked her cheek with it. But my heart was so heavy that I rejected her advances. And as the darkness drew in I began to cry. I wept for a long time, unable to stop, until my chest and throat ached. I wept out of pity for Father and myself, from powerlessness and despair; from the sudden realization that I hadn't the strength to accompany him to the end, and that sooner or later I would turn back and abandon him. I felt as though I were saying farewell to him then, long before our actual parting. Father seemed to sense this: he did not try to comfort me, but sat quietly, deep in thought, every so often stroking my head.

The following morning we set off to visit Fisa. I had sobbed out so much pain that I thought everything would be easier and brighter now. I was prepared in advance to like this dear, unselfish woman who was Father's friend, and who was also apparently 'just the same type as Mama'.

Amidst a thick patch of burdocks on the outskirts of Rokhma a collapsing brick chimney stuck up on top of a decrepit, moss-covered slate roof, and rooted to the ground stood a tiny house. With its crooked little windows and excessively tall chimney it resembled a battered old samovar. Outside the house hung a line of wet washing, so worn and threadbare that no amount of scrubbing could give it back its whiteness. The breeze caught the tattered sails of sheets, which swelled then sank with a damp flap. We entered the house, or rather stepped down into it, as into a shallow pit. The gloomy hall was filled with the stench of the slop bucket, mingled with some other sour, putrid smell. The air in the cramped room seemed quite fresh by comparison. 'So this is the home of Father's love,' I thought, looking around at the miserable iron bed with its mound of grey pillows, the table covered with dark greasy oilcloth, the broken chairs and a shapeless pot-bellied item which had once been either a cupboard or a sideboard.

From behind the cotton curtain dividing off a corner of the room stepped Father's friend, a fairly young woman with light-coloured hair, a large expressionless face and rather prominent growth on her chin. Her grey eyes seemed pleasant, but they gleamed for a mere second before disappearing behind her large, stubborn frontal-bone, and from then until the end of our visit I saw nothing more of Fisa's eyes. I saw nothing of her face, either. She hid everything that could be hidden – her eyes, her face, her hands, her chest, her legs – and exposed only her broad shoulders and her back, bent with toil. I tried in vain to see her as 'Mama's type', as Father had described her, rather than as just an ordinary weaver, like hundreds of others. Yet Father must have seen something in her to have picked her out from all her identical friends. There could be no mistake. This must be what happened to women of 'Mama's type' when oppressed by Rokhma life and the monstrous burdens of poverty, hunger and back-breaking labour.

Rokhma remained every inch true to itself: all my sunny hopes that morning were dashed. Fisa permitted herself not one friendly gesture or kind word, and her occasional abrupt, muttered responses to Father's well-meaning attempts to make us friends were delivered in the same familiar Rokhma tone, rough, rejecting, sullen and secretive, as if to say: 'Don't waste your time.' 'She's shy,' Father whispered to me. I had never seen such an unattractive, inelegant, unsociable creature. At last, after Father had made innumerable shy but unsuccessful enquiries after the samovar, we took our leave of her.

'She's jealous,' said Father on the way home. 'She's afraid my old family will take me away from her.'

I confessed honestly that I hadn't taken to her.

'But didn't you notice how exactly like Mama she is?' Father said in astonishment, quite unoffended. 'Same type as Lily and Elsa, too. I've always loved women like that.' And he started reminiscing about the past.

That evening, rummaging through a pile of books on the table, I found a thick exercise book with a white cover, on which was written: 'Textiliada'. It contained economic formulae, designs of textile machines, diagrams and numerical calculations: Father was evidently mastering a new line of work. I was about to put the book down when my eye was caught by some writing that was much closer to my heart. It was the beginning of a literary article, about the cognition of the world by means of art. I began to read the article, struggling to think who it might be by. The formulations were sharp, clear and compressed, too functional and detached for 'democratic' criticism, and too contemporary for Konstantin Leontiev.

'So you've found my literary efforts?' said Father. He settled down comfortably on the bed, smoking and tapping his ash into the vase which served as his ashtray, and missing. 'I just wanted to develop an idea of Tolstoy's which I don't think has been properly appreciated . . .'

The horror of the 'Closets', all the filth and wretchedness of Rokhma life, the blind beggars and the samovar had left him untouched, as though he were enclosed in an invisible, impenetrable shield. He lived free and untrammelled, sacrificing none of his links with the larger world; having lost everything which forms the basis of life, he had lost nothing of himself. Yet he didn't make a great show of it, and that was why it was so hard for me, callow, anxious and weak-spirited as I was, to see his true greatness.

I thought of this, lying on my hard bed with an extinguished cigarette between my fingers. Father had been asleep a long time, breathing so silently he might have been dead, but the landlady in her flowing garments continued long into the night to dart about the room like a huge bat, tormented by her restless and futile desires.

20

In Moscow

Years passed, the strange formula 'seven and four' ran its course, and Father regained all the rights of a free citizen. Now he could leave Rokhma and travel to Teikovo, or Nerl, or even Shuya – larger towns not being recommended. Now he no longer had to report every month to the district security officer, but only every three months. Now he could spend his holidays where he pleased, with the permission of this same security officer of course. In short, he was free as air. And intoxicated by his new freedom, he set off for Moscow. He had to postpone his trip three times: the district officer didn't want to take the responsibility and referred to the regional officer, who referred in his turn to Moscow. But finally in the spring of 1948, he received permission to leave, and one sunny day in May, Father knocked at the door of our apartment.

We were expecting him. Mama had changed out of her perennial dressing gown into a skirt and cardigan, and had brushed her hair and even put on stockings. Dashura had shaved and was wearing a clean apron. Her face was tearful, but not with the emotion of Papa's return: I had asked her to bake some of that soft bread she used to in the good old days, but in her old age she had forgotten the recipe, and Mama had berated her cruelly for it.

Dashura opened the door, greeted Father and slipped out to the stairs to fetch in his case.

'Hello,' said Mama, going up to him.

'Hello, Katya,' he replied.

They kissed sadly and calmly, like old people for whom everything lay in such a far distant past that there was no point in recalling it, and they didn't want to anyway. They were both silent.

People who meet every day always have something to say to each other, and find every little trifle and drama of their everyday lives important and fascinating. People who haven't seen each other for a decade have nothing to say. The small things are past, and the large things need no words: they are engraved in the grey hairs, the wrinkles and a doglike meekness in the eyes. Meeting again after a very long separation is the same as making a new acquaintance, and they were past the age to make new acquaintances, and too tired.

They had no need to dissemble, or to beg each other's forgiveness for their emotional poverty – the bonds between them were indissoluble, and nothing else was of any significance.

'You've hardly changed at all,' said Father, shocked by the alteration in her face.

She wearily waved her hand.

'And here are some flowers,' he said, handing her a little bunch of yellow and dull-red immortelles.

'How could you bring immortelles into the house!' said Mama. 'They're a bad omen!'

Father, who could never tell one flower from another, had probably thought they were daisies. 'These are all they had . . .' he mumbled shamefacedly.

Mama took the flowers and put them in a vase on top of the wardrobe, where they have remained to this day.

'Would you like a bath?' she asked him. 'Dashura can be making breakfast.'

'Splendid!' said Father, livening up at once. 'How cosy!'

He couldn't light the gas – he had never seen gas in a flat before, and he was childishly delighted when at a turn of a lever a purple flame spurted up and a fine stream of steaming hot water gushed out.

Hardly had we sat down at the table, and Dashura had sullenly served us fried eggs and a burnt loaf not too dissimilar to our favourite soft bread, than there was a knock at the door. Father eyed Mama anxiously, and this glance told me that he must have picked up one or two things from my abject half-truths and evasions.

'Get into the bathroom,' said Mama tersely.

Father scuttled off, and Mama went out into the corridor, closing the door behind her. It was her friend from upstairs, a shrewd, relentlessly inquisitive woman in round spectacles. I don't know what they talked about out there, but Mama didn't let her into the room. She obviously suspected something, and Mother's coldness was to no avail in the face of her friend's burning desire to discover our secret. Finally the front door slammed, and I released Father from his incarceration. The whole crude incident must have been one more wound in his heart.

'Who was that?' Father asked curiously.

'A friend, our upstairs neighbour.'

'Ah, her.' Father didn't go on, but it was all too clear what he meant.

Mother shrugged her shoulders. He still hadn't understood his and our position. He thought we just had to worry about a few spiteful people, rather than having to hide him from everyone.

'We must think of Seryozha,' said Mother with her usual cruel directness. 'They're imprisoning people for no reason again.

Seryozha will deny you, me and the whole damn lot of us if need be.'

'Doesn't Seryozha's wife know I'm here?' Father said tentatively.

Mother goggled at him. 'Are you mad?'

He said nothing and withdrew into himself. Now at last he understood. It was clear that his last lingering illusion had been shattered. He now knew, moreover, of the difficulties of our life, for Mother's brutal honesty had stripped away the slightly insulting tone he'd perceived through all my half-truths. He understood our persecution and our struggles, so much so that when the telephone rang he shot into the bathroom.

Mama stopped him with an irritable gesture: she had said what had to be said, but that made it no less painful for her.

'There's no one at home!' she shouted to Dashura. 'And don't open the door!'

'How am I supposed to do that?' asked Dashura.

'Just don't open it! We don't need a lot of riff-raff in here!'

But things are never all bad in this life. Father's resourceful, sunny nature overcame even this new obstacle. Despite everything, he was in Moscow with the only people he really loved. No one could take this from him. He had traversed a road of unbelievable suffering and endurance and had almost died, but he had survived, he had got here and, however sad his victory, it was a victory none the less. And the delicious home-made fried eggs, and the slightly burnt loaf, and the coffee with cream were a fitting tribute for a conqueror. He became his old lively, funny self again, relaxing at the table as only he knew how to. He drank a cup of coffee, then another, then just one last cup, and then asked, with a comic frightened face, if he might have just one more, his very last.

I looked at Mama, and she smiled at me, a smile of rare and

unguarded warmth. And suddenly I knew that Father's memories of this trip wouldn't be of the loathsome humiliation of running into the bathroom and jumping at every telephone call, but of our devotion to him, however frightened and pitiful it might be.

Of course, Father had pictured his return to Moscow rather differently. He had imagined that he would be surrounded by friends from better times, and that they would have long friendly discussions, tying up the past with the present and giving new meaning to his experiences. But his generation had been savagely thinned: some had died, some had perished in exile, some had been killed in the war. Only a few mohicans survived, and these were such upright, old-fashioned types that there was no reason to prevent Father from seeing them. But his first encounters with them removed his desire to renew these links with the past. The people he met were hopelessly decrepit failures, so crushed by fear as to be almost totally apathetic. Even the most successful of them, a professor with whom Father had had some personal tensions and rivalries as a young man, made such a pathetic impression on him that he came away feeling quite happy.

It saddened yet soothed him. Say what you like, his own fate didn't seem so appalling when you saw these people, living in incomparably better circumstances, who had achieved so little. He was infinitely saddened, however, by the changes in the women, and in this he was utterly selfless. He had an uncanny knack of meeting people on the street, and on his first walk he bumped into one great love and two casual affairs.

'What's happened to Anna Semyovna!' he said with a stricken face.

'The same as happens to all of us – old age,' replied Mother.

'Has Lily changed as much as that, too?' Father asked anxiously.

'As much as that? I may be old and ugly, but I'm a spring chicken compared with Lily. She's a wreck!' said Mother with quiet satisfaction.

It was the end of May, the poplars were in flower, and Father and I decided to take a walk down Gogol Boulevard. He came out of the house first on his own, and I joined him a few minutes later at the corner of Gogol Boulevard and Sivtsev Vrazhek. The fragrance from the trees was so powerful that it drowned out the usual city smells of dust, petrol fumes and asphalt. Downy white fluff drifted through the air and landed on the ground, like shaggy caterpillars.

'There's nothing to beat this smell,' said Father. 'It's only in Moscow that it smells like this.' And with his feeble chest he drew in a great lungful of the fragrant air of his childhood.

We strolled towards Arbat Square, walking so slowly that we were even overtaken by tiny children who had barely learnt to walk. Yet it wasn't such a bad pace if it took Father from the Polar Circle, via Vorkuta and Rokhma, to the poplars of Gogol Boulevard.

21

Before the End

Father now visited Moscow every year, bearing a present from Rokhma of a little bag of hazelnuts picked for me by Fisa's ingratiating daughter. As before, he had to hide in the bathroom whenever anyone paid an unexpected call, but gradually things began to sort themselves out. Necessity makes one pitiless: as his visit approached, we would firmly cut ourselves off from all our friends and acquaintances, without troubling to give them any reasons or explanations, and when the sudden knock came, Mother would ward off the uninvited guest from behind the chained front door. Our friends would be more angry than hurt. They suspected some carefully guarded family secret lurking behind our sudden fits of unsociability, and they hated not knowing what it was. However, we didn't lose a single one of them – tough Soviet types are virtually impossible to offend.

But amongst all our demanding and untrustworthy new friends was a woman of such great emotional integrity that we took the risk of introducing her to Father. My new wife – Nina and I had parted amicably – was someone in whom one could confide anything, and this especially pleased Father with his traditional attitude to marriage and the family. Now he felt truly part of our family circle.

Father did have one last brief and glorious fling. He told us with great animation and humour how he had won the heart of the directress of the textile mill, a woman who was 'absolutely Mama's type'. Rokhma had never seen such a dazzling love affair: he would take his lady to the best restaurant in Ivanovo, and order roast chicken and rice.

This romance cost him his corner in the 'Closets'. His Suzdal landlady, who had more or less come to terms with Fisa on the assumption that she would sooner or later replace her, was deeply upset by the appearance of this formidable new rival. She took to bringing men back to the room, and one of them settled in for good and forced Father to find himself new quarters. He rented a little room at the far end of Rokhma from an old woman who was nicknamed the 'Heart-throb'. The name was quite inappropriate, for the old woman had never made any hearts throb, but her long-dead husband had traded on it. She described his nefarious doings with a strange artlessness and candour. He had robbed travellers on the main highway from Rokhma to Shuya, and had sent quite a few of them to kingdom come. 'He was almost senile, nearly blind and couldn't walk without his stick,' she said, wiping her eyes with the tip of her black, nun-like shawl. 'But he wouldn't give up his work. He'd put on his glasses, grab his stick, and trot, trot . . .' And she would show us how her husband trotted off on his nocturnal business.

Father told us this story in Moscow, and I subsequently heard it from the old woman herself. That was on my last visit to Rokhma.

After Father started spending his annual holidays in Moscow I visited Rokhma less and less, and in the last year and a half I didn't go at all. But then I had to: we had spoken on the telephone and his voice sounded strange and lost. I didn't like the sound of it – not so much muffled as fading away, with none of its old cheerful resonance.

He met me on Zamenhof Square, at the terminus of the bus

line which ran after the war between Rokhma and Ivanovo. The moment I saw him I realized that something was wrong.

On his last visit to Moscow I had given him a smart white summer coat made of rubberized cotton. It suited him very well, and he would peer at his reflection in every mirror and shop window he passed. Now I could barely recognize my gift in the dirty, greasy, tattered rag draped over his body. It was a hot summer day and he didn't really need to wear it, but he had obviously put it on mechanically, not noticing its grimy stains, its greasy collar, or the holes in the places where the buttons had been torn off. What shocked me was not so much the messy appearance of my normally neat father, as some morbid, crushing memory of the past. He had emerged from Saratov looking similarly down-at-heel, but now his neglected appearance was not due to poverty.

'Why are you wearing that filthy thing?' I asked him.

'Yes . . .' he agreed distractedly. 'I should have it cleaned . . .'

The memory of Saratov helped me to understand what had happened to Father. Once again he had lost the strength to bear the burden of loneliness and the constant longing for Moscow, which remained as inaccessible to him as ever. His few brief visits home merely enflamed his homesickness and intensified his despair. The heroic period of his life was over and prosaic reality had set in, without the anguish of suffering, but with the persistent torment of loneliness and regret. He had run out of faith that he would one day leave Rokhma for good and return to Moscow, and with this faith collapsed all his capacity to resist.

Our last meeting in Rokhma was not a cheerful one. Father still asked me about Moscow, the family and our one and only mutual friend, and he even told jokes. He still got up every morning while I was asleep and went to the market to buy something nice, and he still asked me about my latest stories. But everything was tinged with the sadness of a strange detachment. It wasn't that he was cold with me. On the contrary, I had never felt how precious my visit was to him. But he needn't have asked me anything, and I needn't have answered; we could merely have sat smoking together. My presence was all that mattered to him. He cared nothing for my emotional life, only for my physical presence beside him, and I felt chilled and rather appalled by the bloodless being I represented for him.

When he accompanied me to the bus stop, I saw that he was wearing his filthy raincoat again, and I couldn't help wondering if it might be some kind of game. But a glance at his face dispelled any such thought. Of course he hadn't done it on purpose, he had simply stopped taking any notice of his surroundings. He longed for Moscow with every last drop of his strength and intellect. I was no longer merely a son to him, I had become his model of the world he could no longer live without. Now that he was losing this model, he could see neither himself nor anything about him. And looking out of the windows of the bus at the little lost figure in the shapeless, dirty grey garment, I thought: can this really be the end?

No, it wasn't yet the end, but the end was very close.

22

The End

He came to Moscow one more time, quick, restless and younger-looking, in a well-cut coat and suit and a felt hat.

I think he knew then that he was dying, for he asked me to drive him to the riverside walk at Khimki. He wanted to store up some pure, fresh images of the town in which he had been born, had loved and been happy. The town had changed – the houses, the streets, even the names of the streets were different, and so were the people. Since he no longer had any close connection with the town, he turned to the things that had changed least and had guarded his memories most faithfully – to water and trees. He wanted to see the water of the Moscow River, and the trees of Moscow, as golden as in the autumns of his childhood.

We drove to Khimki. He didn't recognize Gorky Street, or the Leningrad Highway, or the Petrovsky Park, but Khimki's station, harbour and granite embankment excited the rapturous admiration he had always felt for the products of human labour. His step became as quick and light as a young man's, and I could barely catch up with him when we walked along the embankment together. Leaves snapped off their stalks, fluttering from the trees on to the water, and floated there.

'That's it, then!' he said, with inexplicable satisfaction, and headed back to the car. Then I suddenly understood – he was settling his accounts. On the way back I spoke to him about myself as I had never spoken to him before. In the past, I had always tried to bolster his confidence by presenting myself as a bold and tireless fighter. Now he needed to know what he was leaving behind on earth. And another thing: he needed to bequeath to someone his unspent energy. The last service on earth which a person can render to those who will live on is to comfort them and inspire them to believe that life isn't so bad. None of this would have been necessary to the punchy, plucky fellow I had always made myself out to be. So on the way back from Khimki I let Father see me as someone on whom he could bestow the final labour of his love.

Throughout the whole of his stay in Moscow he gave the impression of someone embarking upon a new life, whereas in fact he was settling his accounts with the old. All his precarious energy collapsed on the platform of Yaroslavl Station, where my step-father, my wife and I had come to see him off. He lurched past us with strange tottering steps into his carriage, as though he wanted to be done with the agony of the farewell ceremony as quickly as possible. It may have been that his heart was bad, though, and he was hurrying for fear that he wouldn't get there. The pale, yellow skin was stretched tightly over his face, and his eyes were bulging with a look of frightened surprise.

He had come out into the corridor to wave goodbye, when we saw piling into his carriage a gang of rowdy, rather drunk youths from the 'Locomobile' volleyball team, on their way to a match in Ivanovo. They were all strapping, handsome lads, exuding crude energy, and the only reason they didn't push or crush Father was because of the graceful, instinctive agility in their powerful, trained, athletic bodies. Beside these noisy lads, bursting with health, Father's emaciated face, his gasping breath, and the mortal weakness of his tiny frame, seemed so doomed and fragile, so hopelessly played out, that we were all struck by the same thought – that this was the last time we would see him. He must have felt this too, for he hadn't even the strength for a parting smile.

None of us was surprised two and a half months later when a letter from Papa announced that he was ill in hospital. It didn't seem too serious at first, however, and he was soon back at work again. But then he was taken ill again, and this time he lost the use of his right arm.

'The doctors say it's thrombosis,' he told me on the telephone, and asked me to come. I promised to drive over and bring him back to Moscow. The next day I dashed around various motoring offices making enquiries about the route to Ivanovo, and buying a twenty-gallon can of petrol and some spare tyres. Father meanwhile applied for permission to visit Moscow, and was refused. Then the torrential autumn rains set in, the country roads were washed away, and a car journey became out of the question.

This was the start of a terrible game, which even after all these years I find it hard to write about. I kept putting off my trip under a variety of pretexts. I persuaded Father to book into a sanatorium. He followed my advice, and when he left the sanatorium he telephoned again and asked when I was coming. I replied by pronouncing that he must definitely give up work and look after his health properly, that I would send him as much money as he had earned at the factory, and would see to it that he didn't suffer financially. He obediently handed in his resignation from the factory and made an appointment with a specialist in Ivanovo, then rang again to ask me when I would be coming.

But I didn't go. First it was one thing, then another: my own nervous condition, which demanded that I rest, and my writing, which after years of stagnation had suddenly become immensely successful, and I had to build on it. In short, there were any number of good, impressive reasons to be found, all of which were utterly worthless.

Father got plenty of letters from me, and wise, consoling advice, and money for his living expenses, money for his health, money for consultations with the best Ivanovo specialists. But he didn't need any of this. The only thing he needed was for me to go to him.

And I was afraid to go. All my little fears of Rokhma had merged into one huge, despicable fear. It happened as it was bound to happen: I betrayed Father, I hadn't the strength to follow him to the end of his road to Calvary. One more step, one last effort and, although I couldn't have saved him, what I could have given him would have been something close to salvation: the closeness of someone he loved, the illusion of hope, which his trusting heart would have willingly accepted. I did not take that step, I did not make that effort. I deserted him in the face of his imminent death.

I want to end my story about Father with an entry from my diary of 4 April 1952, the day we received the news of his death. In deciding to write the whole truth, I was also trying somehow to justify myself, too. But there was no place for justification in the sharp, pure emotions of that day.

4 April

> This is the end of everything that began on the road to Kandalaksha, when I had just rediscovered that poignant, imperious, rarely uttered word 'Father'. Most people's fathers are the most powerful basis of their lives. Mine was different: gentle, suffering and shunning the slightest violence. I owe him far more gratitude than other sons owe the fathers who have fed, clothed and educated them. I fed, clothed and educated him – there at least my con-

science is clear. But thanks to him I have known more suffering than I shall know in all the rest of my life. The shabbiness and cruelty it has left behind has formed the basis of all my emotional experiences. The little figure behind the barbed wire of the camp, the little figure on the Rokhma highway, his determination to walk 'as far as that telegraph pole', the way he gazed after me when I left, a look I felt so physically that I wanted to hide from it – all this was so incomparably greater than anything that even the best father could give his son.

Yet how could one give the name of 'Father' to that tiny little man, so weak and vulnerable, who only came up to my shoulder? He gave me life, and I settled up with him for that. When he was sick, semi-naked, dying of starvation and with almost no flesh on him, he came to spend his last days in Rokhma. There I fed and clothed him, and gave him life. That was all that was required of me then. And if he became human again, capable of working, reading books, being happy and loving women, it was my doing. It was as though I had given birth to him anew by a conscious effort of love, pity and anger. He was my son – that is why there can be no forgiveness for me now. When the son betrays his father, that is as it should be; sooner or later, all children betray their parents. But there is no forgiveness for the father who betrays his son, and that is what I did. I betrayed my son when he was old, sick, lonely and dying . . .